While the Baby Sleeps
Stephanie Hazeltine

WHILE THE BABY SLEEPS

Edited: Laura Boon at It's All Write

Cover design: Elle at Elle Maxwell Design

Published by Hazeltine Publishing

Ebook: 978-0-6455756-2-0

Paperback: 978-0-6455756-3-7

To Grandma,
Thank you for inspiring and encouraging me to write

In memory of Old Grandie,
One of my first storytellers

Note to my readers:

This book deals with topics including domestic violence, post-natal depression and suicide.

Prologue

I'd only spent a short time learning his routine. I wasn't even sure what I was hoping to achieve by following him. Maybe just confront him and tell him to leave, but I'd become more desperate. It was a chilly night. A cool change moved in late in the evening and brought with it a downpour of summer rain. I was rugged up from head to toe—black puffer jacket, black beanie and gloves. I blended into the night landscape.

He never saw me coming.

I hadn't meant for this to happen though. It wasn't premeditated, as they'd say on the cop shows. But as I followed him, images from my past flashed before me. A calmness took over. I knew what I had to do.

The blow was fast.

He was jogging, like he didn't have a care in the world. As though he had no idea how many lives he was destroying. So, when he stopped for a moment to check his phone, something in me snapped.

He tapped away at his screen. He couldn't hear me with those headphones on. Then I lifted the cricket bat and knocked him for six. He fell instantly.

Now, I look down at my gloved, shaking hands, splattered with blood. Lying at my feet is a cricket bat, a fitting weapon. Not planned as such. But the bat was lying on the backseat of the car, and I didn't feel safe going into the parklands at this hour with nothing at all.

Next to the bat, his unblinking eyes stare up at me. A pool of crimson spreads out from underneath his head and mixes with the puddles of muddy water.

I take a deep breath to calm my shaking body. I look around. It's hard to see far at this time of night. Only a few distant lampposts cast light on the parklands. I'd be surprised to find anyone else out here at this time or in this weather. There aren't many people like him who mess with the normality of day and night.

I pick up the bat and leave. There is nothing else that ties me to this incident and the bat will be easy to chop up and add to the Coonara. I take one last look back at the body and then break into a jog.

It'll be okay, I keep telling myself.

Chapter 1

Amalia

It is some sort of phenomenon that the moment a parent steps into the shower, they're certain they hear their baby crying. I'd read about it on Facebook groups and in the baby app I'd been using since I was pregnant. Lila has finally fallen asleep, and I jump at the opportunity to wash my hair before I go out later. Then I hear the cries. I turn off the running water and poke my head out the bathroom door into my bedroom where I left her sleeping soundly in her bassinet. She's still there, sound asleep. *Of course.*

The anticipation of the next phantom cry forces me to wash my hair at frantic speed, and I step out of the shower to find a big clump of conditioner still in my hair. I wipe it away with my towel and find something to wear. But what do you wear to your first mothers' group session? In my head, mothers' group is just an opportunity for women to compare themselves and their babies. She's lost more baby weight than me. She's exclusively breastfeeding; what's wrong with my boobs? How did she manage to do her hair like that with a baby around? Why is her baby rolling while my blob doesn't move? I realise I'm being super judgy and my theory probably stems from watching too much reality TV, but still, I'm nervous.

It's not only the prospect of feeling like a failure in comparison to other mums though. I've put a lot of pressure on these sessions and what they could evolve into. This is my opportunity to make friends, to create a bond like my mum had. Boy, do I wish she was here now. Not only to give me the kick in the butt I need to get out there and meet people, but for every single other thing in my life.

How did she do it as a single mum? How did she pull herself together after Dad's accident to care for me? Like her, I didn't choose to be a single mum, but here I am in the same position. I desperately wish she was here to give me advice. Like what TOG sleeping bag do I put on Lila when it's a hot day? I'd never even heard of TOG ratings before Lila was born. Mum probably didn't even pay attention when I was a baby. I wish I could ask her how long it took me to learn to latch when she was breastfeeding, or how long it took for me to stop crying for what appeared to be absolutely no reason. Would she be able to tell me if Lila's projectile spews are normal or if there is something wrong with her? I would give anything to have her here. But instead, I will follow her dying wish and that means getting dressed and going to this mothers' group.

I put on a pink and white maxi dress that buttons down the front to allow easy access for Lila to feed and is flowy enough to hide what still looks like a pregnant belly. Lila continues to sleep soundly. I even manage to blow dry my hair, which is a welcome change from the wet mum-bun that is usually fastened on top of my head after a shower and stays there until it's washed again. My long brown hair comes away in chunks in my hand. I'd read about postpartum hair loss, but my hair was so thick, I was looking forward to it becoming more manageable. Although, I am sick of picking clumps of it out of the shower drain and off the floor, and once from Lila's nappy. *How?*

I make myself a cup of coffee and sit down to take a sip. Right on cue, Lila cries out. I can't complain. I'm dressed, my hair is washed and dried, and my coffee will still be there when I feed her.

I take Lila to her bedroom. She still sleeps next to my bed. I actually like having another person in the bedroom again. It was lonely those last few months of pregnancy being on my own. I pick out a cute little romper in a mustard colour that has a matching bow.

'We're going to make some new friends today, sweetheart,' I say to her, and she looks up at me from her change table, totally unaware of what I said. 'Well, I hope so anyway.'

As I feed Lila and drink my lukewarm coffee, I imagine what the other mums will be like. I wonder if I've seen any of them around town before. It's not a huge town, but I don't get out much. Not anymore anyway. I wonder if I'll be the only single mum. Will they pity me? Gosh, I hope they don't pity me.

When Lila finishes her feed, I load her into the pram, and we set off for the community centre.

I can do this.

Chapter 2

Marnie

'Where are my bloody keys?' I say aloud to no one. Well, not no one. My eight-week-old son looks up at me from his capsule on the living room floor, totally useless when it comes to key recovery.

I rummage through the nappy bag—a recent addition to my life that I don't love. It's like a bottomless pit of junk. So many items for 'just in case'. Nappies and wipes I can understand. But then there are backup bottles, dummies, booties, spare bibs, spare clothes, toys, teethers (do they even get teeth this early?). But it's all packed. Every time I leave the house, it's as though I'm headed for the desolate wilderness and will be stranded with a naked, starving, teething baby.

As I dig through the supplies, searching for my keys, one of the straps knocks my Keep Cup and the contents tips onto my cream linen dress. Liquid gold. My best friend. Coffee gone, and I don't have time to make another one, especially now I have to change. I consider shooting a frantic text to my husband, Rob, as I teeter on the edge of a breakdown. I'm tempted to bail on one of the only outings I've planned since having Jasper. But I know he'll either be too busy to respond or he'll tell me to get over it and get out there.

Taking a deep breath, I rush to the laundry. Jasper will be okay for a minute. I rip off the dress and throw it in a bucket to soak. In the bedroom, I pull on my trusty leggings and feeding singlet—the same items of clothing I've worn for almost two months. On my way back to the living room, I spy my keys under the table. They must have escaped my Mary Poppins bag of chaos.

'Alright, kiddo. Let's do this.'

It's only a five-minute drive to the Lakesfield Community Centre, but that's more than enough time for my usual anxiety to kick in. Heavy chested and suddenly desperate for the toilet, I pull into the carpark and grip the steering wheel tightly. My knuckles whiten as I take ten deep breaths in and out, like I've been told to do many times by various psychologists. Before Jasper came along, it was nerves about my work as a teacher, driving in the rain or travelling overseas. Now it's everything and it's all the time. I keep being reminded to meditate, perhaps do some mindful colouring. I don't have time to pee on my own, let alone pick up a pencil. But I take a moment to breathe and let my heart rate settle.

There are a few other mums already pushing their prams into the centre. The clock on the dash says 10:55am. I've still got five minutes before my first mothers' group session. A million thoughts race through my head. *Will I be the oldest? Will they notice how much I'm struggling? Will they judge me for it?*

I'm a thirty-eight-year-old first-time mum, not through lack of trying in my younger years. Rob and I eventually had Jasper—our miracle—through IVF. But from the moment he arrived, I've worried. Worried about his health, his weight, his wellbeing, his feeding, his sleeping, everything. So far, I haven't enjoyed being a mum. The most recent psychologist, the one the hospital recommended I see after an emotional home visit with a midwife, says it's all normal. But then why is every second mum on Instagram posting adorable, happy snaps with captions like #mumlife and #blessed?

Jasper gives a little cry from his capsule in the back. Of course, the car has stopped moving and he has noticed. There's never a moment of peace. I take out the pram and wrestle with it as though it's some sort of wild crocodile. The shop assistants bang on about how easy this one or that one is to assemble. Every single pram I tried seemed to pinch my fingers or kick out onto my toes. I'll master it someday. I strap Jasper in, as another mum does the same thing alongside me.

'Hey. First mothers' group?' she asks, her voice far too bright and cheery.

She has long blonde hair, styled into stunning waves that fall around her made-up face. How does she have time for that with a baby? I self-consciously play with the loose hairs falling from my messy mum-bun.

'Yep,' I respond, trying to sound more confident than I feel.

'Me too. Can't wait to meet everyone,' she beams. 'And their little bubbas,' she adds and gushes at Jasper in his pram. 'Who's this little guy?'

A freshly painted nail tickles Jasper's little foot. *Painted nails.* I rarely have time to brush my teeth or put on deodorant, let alone have a manicure.

'This is Jasper. I'm Marnie.'

The woman pulls me in for a hug and I'm completely taken by surprise.

'Sorry,' she says as she pulls away, 'I'm a hugger. My name's Fleur and this is Mia.' She lifts the hood on her pram and a bright-eyed, baby girl stares up at me. 'I'll see you in there.'

I finish packing the desert-island-survival-kit-for-babies into the bottom of my pram. Fleur trots away in her high-heeled wedges, but not before stopping for a selfie with Mia outside the centre. The way her gorgeous, floral wraparound dress fits makes it look like she has never given birth, at least not recently. I will myself not to be so judge-mental or jealous. She seems lovely and she's probably a nice person.

Plus, I'm new to the area, so I need to be open to making friends. I lock the car and head inside.

When I enter, there's one seat remaining in a circle. It's next to Fleur. She smiles and waves me over. There are six of us in total, each with a pram in tow. There's also a much older woman sitting with a pile of leaflets and a doll on her lap. The room feels old. I imagine it's barely had more than a lick of paint since us mothers were babies ourselves. Below a row of windows, there's a bench with a few change mats. The change mats have yellowed over time, made obvious by their white undersides. Covering most of the walls are posters with curled up corners that show graphics and fonts from the old Microsoft Word Art and Clip Art. Those were the simple days, before graphic design was suddenly added to us teachers' ever-growing list of necessary skills. There are a few pieces of play equipment in one corner. Opposite the windows are two doors. I guess they're the offices they use for us to meet one-on-one with the nurses. The offices where I've been told they bombard you with questions and send you home with a hundred more questions of your own.

'Okay, I think we're all here,' the older woman says. 'I'm Liz, your group's facilitator and one of the local maternal health nurses. I recognise a few of you from some earlier appointments.'

I haven't seen Liz before. But then, I also haven't been here to the community centre with Jasper before now. A lovely nurse has been doing our check-ups at home, very aware of how much I struggle to leave the house. Getting here today is a monumental achievement.

'We'll begin by going around the circle and introducing ourselves.'

Argh. I hate ice-breaker exercises like this. The school I worked at insisted that we do them with the kids on the first day of school. I could always feel their awkwardness and nerves as they tried to recite their name, favourite hobby and something they looked forward to while also maintaining a 'cool' image for their new classmates. Now, it's my turn to feel awkward and nervous. I'm sure as hell not going to appear cool. I count my breaths again in my head.

'Tell us your name, your baby's name and how old your baby is,' Liz continues. 'Let's start with you.' She turns to the woman to her immediate left and I'm flooded with relief knowing I don't have to go first.

A young-looking girl with beautiful red hair smiles shyly. 'I'm Peyton and this is Lucas.' She turns Lucas around on her lap so that we can see his little face. 'He's ten weeks old.' Lucas has the same red hair as his mum and he smiles right on cue.

Liz motions to the next woman in the circle.

The woman is breastfeeding. She has dark hair that's braided messily down her back. 'Hi, I'm Zara. And this little boob monster here is Tiana. She's almost eight weeks old.' Zara feeds with ease and confidence. Not like me. I'm constantly squirming and adjusting something, usually resulting in me flashing a nipple and squirting anyone who comes too close.

Fleur is next, and she introduces twelve-week-old Mia, who turns out to be our oldest baby. I introduce Jasper and somehow I get through the sentence without my voice wavering.

I turn to my left to see the next woman as she introduces herself. 'I'm Amalia. This is Lila. She's seven weeks old.' Amalia speaks extremely softly and hides behind a curtain of her long, brown hair.

The last woman introduces herself. 'Hey, I'm Hanbi and this is nine-week-old Sienna.' Hanbi oozes confidence and I'm immediately intimidated by her. Her black slacks and white buttoned shirt makes her look as though she came straight from the office. Surely nobody is back at work yet? I can barely manage a daily shower.

Liz runs through a whole lot of services available to us in the area and loads up our prams with handfuls of leaflets and freebies. I spy titles on brochures saying things like 'Safe Sleeping' and 'Pets and Babies' and inwardly sigh. More information to overload my already jam-packed brain. As if social media and Google aren't enough, now I've got some good-old-fashioned reading to do to send my anxiety levels into a frenzy.

'So, for this session, our focus is on feeding. You don't have to share anything, but this is an open discussion for you to talk about your feeding journey or ask any questions you may have about feeding your baby. Who would like to go first?'

I avoid eye contact with Liz. I'm certainly not keen on sharing my story, let alone speaking first.

'I will!' Zara shouts, followed by a giggle. 'Obviously I'm breast-feeding.' She looks down at Tiana who's still attached to her. 'It hasn't been totally smooth sailing, but you know 'breast is best' and what-ever, so I kept at it, and now we're doing great.'

I roll my eyes and hope no one notices. *Breast is best.* Three of the most deflating, damaging, dangerous words a mum can hear. Since having Jasper, I've learnt that there are about a million best ways to care for and raise your child, and every expert has a different reason why their way is best. It's only been eight weeks, but my way is survival mode. I breastfeed, which I consider myself lucky to do. But I don't always cope with it. Sometimes Rob will give a bottle of expressed milk if there's any, or some formula. The nurse who visits me at home was quick to correct the saying and tell me 'fed is best', and that's how I get by. Survival mode.

It's as if Liz reads my mind. 'I'm so pleased you've been able to breastfeed, Zara.' She turns to the group. 'While nobody can deny the benefits of breastmilk, please don't beat yourself up if you aren't having the same experience. I disagree with the sentiment that 'breast is best'. We want to support you in giving your child enough food so that they gain a healthy amount of weight, but it has to be what's best for you and your family. Your health, especially your mental health, is most important.' *Hell yeah, Liz.*

Zara blushes before flicking her braids behind her shoulder.

'However, Zara, you said you didn't always find it easy. What strategies did you use to help with your breastfeeding?'

Zara sits up taller. 'Well, for one, lactation cookies helped with my supply. I've got a great recipe if anyone wants it.'

'What a load of crap.'

Everyone looks at Hanbi, a little shocked. The blunt outburst is so at odds with her sophisticated corporate look.

'What?' Hanbi shrugs. 'I don't believe those cookies work. They didn't for me, anyway. Besides, I'm not always available to feed Sienna. Luckily, she loves a bottle.'

Zara strokes Tiana's head as she continues to nuzzle at her breast. 'My Tiana isn't interested in a bottle.'

Hanbi purses her lips.

I worry about how this group is going to make me feel each week. You hear about mothers' groups that get competitive or bitchy. I hope that isn't the case here.

Liz cuts in before we have a full-on debate in our first session. 'Any other tips, Zara?'

'We also do a lot of skin-to-skin time and we co-sleep, which makes it easier for me to feed her on demand.'

Zara is like every Instagram meme about breastfeeding that makes me think I'm the world's worst mother. I take comfort in the fact that no one else is nodding along. It's not that I have an issue with her methods. I don't. But breastfeeding isn't easy or enjoyable for everyone. Co-sleeping isn't everyone's cup of tea, certainly not mine. My marriage is strained enough without adding a living physical barrier to the bed.

Liz steers the conversation in a more inclusive direction and almost everyone shares a tiny insight into the way they feed their babies. I'm relieved when I hear I'm not the only one mixed feeding. The only mum who doesn't share with the group is Amalia. She listens quietly, rocking a sleeping Lila in her arms.

Chapter 3

Peyton

Lucas screams the entire way home from the community centre. I wish I'd stayed home. I'm relieved to pass him over to Mum when I walk in the front door.

'How was the first mothers' group session?' she asks and takes Lucas in her arms. 'Shhh, shhh, shhh,' she bounces him up and down.

'Boring, as expected. Should've stayed home to be honest.' I grab a wine glass and an open bottle of chardonnay from the fridge. I'd much prefer a cider or vodka seltzer, but I'll take whatever's on offer in mum's fridge.

'Bit early for that, isn't it?'

The clock on the kitchen wall says 12:25.

I shrug. 'It's after midday. Besides, you said you'd have Lucas tonight so I could go out.'

Mum lets out an exasperated sigh. 'Yes, of course I'll watch him. Tonight. But he's your responsibility until then.'

I wait for her to add the standard *'I wish you'd grow up'* line that she so often uses, but it doesn't come. I take my glass of wine to the table outside. Summer is finally living up to its name, and I need to get some colour into my pasty skin. Mum finds a shadier spot at the table and sits with a now calm Lucas in her arms. He always settles down for her, and a pang of jealousy shoots through me.

The palms make shadows over the pool that I love spending my summers next to. I used to lay there sunbathing for hours on the lounges, reading magazines or listening to music. The doctor had only recently given me the all clear to go swimming again, and even though I can, there's no time. I tried recently. Lucas fell asleep so I quickly put my bikini on and lathered myself in sunscreen. I love a tan, but I'm always strict with the sunscreen. Nothing worse than peeling skin, plus I don't rate the leathery look older women sport in middle age. By the time I grabbed a towel and set up outside with a podcast, the monitor flashed and Lucas' cries broke my peace. I haven't bothered trying again.

'So, tell me all about it. Were the other mums nice?' Mum breaks my daydream.

'Sure.'

'Anyone you get along with especially?'

I shake my head. 'Not really. They're all much older than me and you know I don't especially get along with other girls.'

I never had many girlfriends in school, either. I haven't kept in contact with anyone from last year. But I suppose my life took an unusual turn compared to the rest of my graduating class.

'Well, you're only nineteen. I'm not surprised you're the youngest. But I'm sure there must be some other young mums that you can get to know there.'

I think about the group. Zara with her breastfeeding guilt trip. *No thanks*. Marnie looked Mum's age. Pretty sure Hanbi came on her lunch break from work. Fleur was annoyingly cheerful and Amalia barely said a word.

'Sure. Maybe.' I lie.

Lucas grizzles.

'He needs a feed,' Mum says, looking down at him.

I look at my empty wine glass. 'Give him a bottle.'

'Peyton!'

'What?' Of course I know what. I'm being lazy and bratty, but I don't want to parent twenty-four seven. It's hard.

'I don't care if you don't want to breastfeed your child.' She glances at my wine glass, disapproval written all over her face. 'But you will feed your child. Get the bottle yourself, and you can take him inside for it.'

After storming inside, I warm up a bottle of formula. I know I'm acting like a spoiled teenager. I suppose I am a spoiled teenager. Knocked up at eighteen by a guy who wants nothing to do with me. I couldn't bring myself to terminate the pregnancy, and Mum and Dad offered to help me out. They said I was welcome to keep living here and they'd support me and my baby. I don't regret having Lucas. But I can't help but feel sorry for myself some days when I see pictures on social media of old friends partying, moving away for uni and travelling the world.

Mum brings Lucas inside and I take him from her and sit on the couch. I stare at him as he guzzles from the bottle eagerly. His green eyes are bright, like the father he'll never know, but the rest of him is me. He has my red hair, lots of it already, and pale skin. Mum keeps showing me photos of me at Lucas' age and the resemblance is incredible.

'Are you having anymore?' Mum holds up my wine glass.

I look back down at Lucas and my insides feel warm in a way that alcohol can't make me feel. 'No, thanks.'

I stay on the couch for the next two hours as Lucas finishes his bottle, and he sleeps in my arms. I watch his adorable, pouty, little lips move as he breathes in and out. It's not summer in Ibiza, but it's pretty damn satisfying.

***

Mum has been worried about me since I had Lucas. She's been on my back about reconnecting with school friends or joining different groups to make new friends. I've never had a best friend. At school, I mostly played sports or hung out with the guys. I knew they found me attractive, and I liked the attention they gave me. The girls tended to not like me for all the same reasons. When one of those boys got me pregnant at the end of the school year, I was damaged goods. I did my exams and then basically vanished off the face of the earth.

If I ask Mum to watch Lucas, she basically pushes me out the door every time hoping that the shopping trip or night out will be the time I find a friend, a boyfriend or anyone willing to talk to a nineteen-year-old mum living with her parents.

I hadn't made any plans specifically for tonight, but I knew I'd be keen for a drink after the mothers' group session. I only went because Mum wouldn't stop nagging me, but a part of me hoped maybe there'd be another mum there that I could start a friendship with. From first glance, I don't think there is. But Liz gave out some freebies, and I learnt a few things, so I'll give it another go.

The cricket club always has a social night on a Thursday after training. I used to go with my family when my brother played. He lives interstate now, but I still like to go to matches on the weekend and some social nights. I know I can go down there, have a drink with the locals, and forget about everything else. I haven't been since I fell pregnant though. How would I explain why I wasn't drinking?

I hook my breast pump up to both sides and hold it in place with a crop top so I can do my hair and makeup at the same time. I'm glad I didn't have that second glass of wine earlier so I can actually use this liquid gold—pouring it down the sink is painful. I scroll through Spotify trying to find some tunes to drown out the rhythmic humming of the pump. *Noughties Top Hits*—that'll do. 'Independent Women' by Destiny's Child comes through the Bluetooth speaker in the bathroom. How fitting.

I bottle up the milk I've collected. It should be enough to get Lucas through until tomorrow, when I'm sober enough to give him the real thing. Man, I'm sick of counting my drinks. Isn't nine months sober long enough? I should be entering my peak partying phase, not recording my drinks in some safety app. Although I stopped doing that after a few weeks and grabbed a tin of formula. Judge away, but I'm nineteen.

Ignoring my ugly maternity bra, I put on a hot lacy one and stuff it with breast pads—less hot. Then I throw on a high-waisted mini skirt and cute crop. I've always been athletic, and pregnancy didn't slow me down. I quite enjoy seeing the surprise on someone's face when I tell them I have a newborn baby and they see this body. Admiring my outfit in the mirror, I do a little twirl. I'm happy with it.

I grab my purse and keys out of the nappy backpack, and they join my phone in a little shoulder bag. So nice to leave the house without carrying half of Baby Bunting on my back.

Mum is feeding Lucas the pumped milk. Well, trying to. He's dozing off and not drinking.

I sneak over. 'Goodnight, my handsome boy.' I give him a peck on his forehead. 'Thanks Mum, see ya.' I kiss her on the cheek.

'Don't be too late, Peyton. I'm not home in the morning and Lucas doesn't understand sleep ins.'

I roll my eyes. 'Yes, Mum.'

When I get to the cricket club, it's still light. Thank you daylight savings! The sun sinks slowly on the other side of the oval. It's a warm night, so most people are out on the deck of the clubhouse having a drink. I grab a cider and sit at a high table with a group of older guys. They've all known me since I was a kid, and they all know I want to sit here, people watch and enjoy a few drinks. It's what I love about coming here. I can take my spot at a table, and I don't have to make conversation. No pretending to be someone else. I can relax.

A few of the guys smile and mutter hello as I take a seat, but otherwise, they continue their own conversations. My cold drink creates a ring of water on the table that seeps onto a flyer. I pick it up and shake off the drops that have stained one corner. *Fluoro Night*, the flyer reads. I shake my head. So lame. The club is always hosting themed nights to raise money. There's always a small entry fee, and then people donate food and prizes, and they draw you in with the promise of one free, fancy drink.

'Sounds fun, right?'

I look up from the flyer. It's Bree. Her brother is the same age as mine and they played together from juniors until recently. We used to hang out during every match and at every social event, but not so much anymore. We're different. I like drinking, dressing up and boys. She likes reading, studying and being boring. I'm surprised to see her out on a uni night, and she looks different. It's been a while, but she's ditched the daggy jeans and polo for clothes I'd almost consider wearing myself. She looks...pretty.

'Bree, hey. Yeah, standard fundraiser, I guess. I haven't seen you in ages.'

'I haven't been at the club in a while. Quit uni, did some travelling, and now I'm back. Hashtag-new-me or whatever.'

I inwardly cringe. I hate when people use hashtags in conversation.

'So, are you going to come Saturday then?' she asks.

I look back at the flyer. Shit, it's this weekend. I wonder if Mum will have Lucas again so soon. Maybe if I tell her I've made a friend she'll agree.

'Yeah, maybe.'

Bree jumps up and down and squeals. Such an overreaction. 'Yay! Well, don't forget your fluoro outfit. We'll catch up properly then.'

I put the flyer back on the table, away from the pool of water my glass has made. Clearly I'm not drinking it fast enough if the ice is melting this quickly. I down the rest without taking a breath and go inside to the bar.

The thought of hanging out with Bree, even if she has changed, isn't super enticing. But then, spending Saturday night with a baby attached to my boob isn't that much better. I'll ask Mum tomorrow.

The bar inside is getting busier now that more people have knocked off work. I take my spot in line while I scroll through Instagram. Not looking where I'm going, I bump into the guy in front of me.

He turns around.

I glance up for a split second and put my hand up. 'Sorry,' I murmur.

Then I look up again quickly, giving him a full body double take. This guy earned his double take. He is hot. I've never seen him at the club before. He's tall, broad and, from the way his muscles look in his cricket training gear, he's fit. He has dark hair with sprinkles of grey and the most stunning green eyes. I'd guess he'd be in his thirties or maybe (looking exceptionally good) early forties. His skin is bronzed from the sun, and there are tan lines at his ankles where his socks usually are.

'No worries,' he says and smiles.

My face warms. That smile, wow. I silently thank the concealer that's hiding my red cheeks right now.

Jake, the bartender, grabs his attention, and he turns away from me. He takes his beer and heads outside. I watch him a little too closely. My eyes planted firmly on his tight ass and toned calves.

'Peyton.' Jake is tapping his hand on the bar.

'Sorry, another cider. Thanks Jake.'

I go back to my spot at the table. It's cooler now, so a couple of the gas heaters around us have fired up. I watch the people around me, like I always do. There are the mums sipping their wines between telling off their tired kids who want to go home. The guys standing around are discussing the upcoming match and team selection. The hot guy from the bar is with the captain of the firsts and a couple of other players. He's shaking their hands, as though he's just meeting them. They all wear the same navy training gear, so I wonder if today was his first session. That'd explain why I've never seen him before.

If he's new here, what better way to meet people than a social function? I glance at the flyer on the table. Hanging out with Bree might not be that tempting, but seeing this guy again is. I put the flyer in my bag, sit back and enjoy my evening free of nappies, milk and a crying baby.

Chapter 4

Fleur

Mothers' group was amazing. It's just so nice to meet some other cool mums, and Mia made some cute friends. I love hearing birth stories and feeding stories and sharing this journey with other women. Women empowering women, right?

These are the thoughts running through my head as I drive home from the centre.

Shut up, Fleur. No one's here. You don't have to pretend anymore.

Pulling up at our rundown two-bedroom unit on the outskirts of town, I sigh before lugging everything inside. I hate this house. I pop Mia in the bouncer on the floor of our drab living room. The poor girl deserves better than this. I wrestle off the Spanx that were holding every curve in perfect position and swap them for activewear. I tie my hair back up in its rightful place on top of my head. That was the first time it's been styled in months. I thought the more together I looked, the more together I'd seem. I think they bought it. As I untie the wrap dress I found cheap on Facebook marketplace, I catch sight of myself in the mirror. My back is like a timeline of yellowing bruises fading from last week to deep purple ones fresh from yesterday. I throw on a feeding singlet and lift Mia from her bouncer.

'Time for some lunch, sweetheart.'

When Mia finishes feeding, she usually naps for a few hours in the afternoon. I know I'm lucky she sleeps so well. But there's none of this *sleep while the baby sleeps* crap going on in this house. When Mia sleeps, I work my butt off. Aaron will be home in a few hours, there's washing and housework to do, and he asked for a roast dinner tonight.

I don't know where Aaron thinks we can get the money to make fancy roast dinners, or any of the other lavish requests he makes, but I know better than to argue. There are some questionably old veggies in the fridge that'll do the trick once roasted, so I chop them up. We certainly don't have any meat, but the local grocer will put their last few hot chooks on sale late this afternoon, so I'll pick up one of those later.

I potter around the house, tidying up the mess from getting dressed up this morning. The makeup I rarely use is spread out across the bathroom bench. I clean it up and wipe what's left of it off my face as well. Scrubbing off the red nail polish I quickly splashed on this morning, I wonder if anyone even noticed. I'm surprised I even had nail polish in the house. My theory was that no one would suspect the perfectly made-up, manicured mum of being in trouble. Mia stirs, so I creep down the hall to her room to listen. Maybe she'll settle herself and sleep a little longer. The hallway isn't long, but I've tried to fill every space with photos to make the poky old house a little homier. Opposite Mia's room is a photo of Aaron and me from our wedding day six years ago. We got married young. A couple of twenty-two-year-old high school sweethearts, thinking we were the luckiest people in the world. We hadn't seen the real world yet.

We rented in a suburb close to the Melbourne CBD and spent our weekends brunching and partying with our friends. We had a small, cheap wedding because being married was all that mattered to us, despite both our parents' pleas to wait a few years. Aaron studied and became an accountant and I trained to be a nurse. In between semesters, we travelled the world on a shoestring budget we saved from various casual jobs. We honestly lived the best life.

When Aaron graduated and started a new job at a big city firm, things changed. He was mixing with wealthy people and nothing we had was ever good enough. He started to gamble because he thought that was the best way to get rich quick. *Idiot.* Before we knew it, Aaron had lost his job, we were in debt and the only place we could afford to live was a small town an hour out of Melbourne. It was, somehow, my fault.

Now, Aaron works at a small accounting agency in town, earning half of what he earned in the city. When we moved here, he started drinking every night. I was heartbroken and began to think our parents were right. Despite our change in circumstances, Aaron still had high expectations. I always had to look good. We still had to have good meals. The house had to appear perfect, despite its size and location. Then, two years ago, he forgot my birthday. He got home from work in the afternoon and saw some flowers on the bench from a friend and a card wishing me a happy birthday and he lost it. Apparently, I should've reminded him my birthday was coming up. That was the first night he hit me. *Happy birthday, Fleur.*

That night, in bed, he apologised and held me. Promised me it would never happen again. He was my high school sweetheart. Of course I believed him. I loved him, and foolishly, I still do.

Things didn't improve for about a year and I thought a baby might help. Aaron sounded excited by the idea, and it gave me so much hope. It didn't take long for me to fall pregnant. Aaron didn't lay a hand on me for the entire nine months and I knew we'd made the right decision.

But when Mia was one week old, the endless, typical crying of a newborn kept us up all night. It was my fault. And every day since it's been my fault. I'm not feeding her enough, she's not warm enough, I don't play with her enough. I have bruises to remind me to do better.

I poke my head into Mia's room and her eyes are wide open. There's no settling her this time. I strap her into the car seat and drive back into town. It's a small enough town that everything is nearby but big enough that not everyone knows everyone. Thank goodness, otherwise mothers' group would've been awkward. I don't want them to know that I live in the dodgy house on the outskirts of town or that my husband is the one they see strolling home drunk on Saturdays.

I grab a hot roasted chicken; the smell makes my mouth water. Aaron will love it, surely. All these years later, I'm still giddy when I think of ways to make him happy. Pathetic, I know. On my way back to the car, I stop by the bottle shop and pick up a bottle of his favourite red. I tap my card and it beeps with approval. I inwardly sigh, thankful those parental leave payments have started.

When I get home, I put Mia on her play mat with some toys. She holds one above her head and drops it clumsily to her face. Then does it all over again. I take the moment of peace to get the veggies in the oven and start some gravy. I lay the table and even light a candle. Aaron usually gets home at about six. I glance at the oven clock: 5:30. I'm excited about all the effort I've made so I bath Mia early with the hope that we can put her to bed and enjoy our dinner alone.

At six o'clock, Aaron barges in, muttering something about the bins being left out. *Oops. Knew I forgot something.*

'Where's Mia? Ready for her bath?'

'Well actually,' I smile. 'Mia's had her bath. I've gotten her to sleep so we can enjoy a roast dinner, just us.' I try to make my voice sound sexy, as though I've organised some amazing date night, but it comes out shaky.

'You what?' He slams his fist on the kitchen bench. 'You know bathing Mia is my thing. And what? Now she's asleep. So I don't even get to see my daughter today?'

He's yelling, and I take a step back.

'Sorry babe, I thought you'd be tired, and we could relax, have a date night.'

He storms off towards Mia's room, muttering loud enough for me to hear. 'Bloody selfish. Keeping my daughter from me.'

Dinner will help things, but I feel deflated. I watch on the monitor as Aaron sneaks into Mia's room and gives her a kiss goodnight. I hold my breath, hoping she doesn't wake up. For all his flaws, he loves Mia.

Aaron slumps on the couch near the kitchen and flicks on the television. I potter around the kitchen putting the finishing touches on our meal while he scrolls mindlessly on his phone.

'What the hell is this?' he yells, and I jump, sloshing gravy on the backsplash. He's holding his phone up, so the screen is facing my direction.

It's a photo of Mia and me outside the community centre this afternoon. I wasn't going to go to all the effort of doing my hair and makeup and wearing bloody Spanx without documenting it on Instagram.

'Oh, that's from our first mothers' group today.' I wait for the compliment.

'And you're dressed like *this* to impress who exactly?'

My stomach drops. He's angry, again.

'I thought it would be nice to dress up to meet some new mums in the area.'

He walks into the kitchen. 'Thought it would be nice, huh? And then you come home, and *this* is what you wear for me.' His mouth curls in disgust at my food stained activewear and mum-bun. 'Didn't you call this a date night?'

I fight back the tears. 'I can get changed now. I didn't want to get messy while I was cooking,' I lie.

'Don't bother. Anyway, why are you in a mothers' group? I don't want any nosy, gossipy cows around my kid.'

'No, they were nice. It'll be great for Mia to meet some other babies.'

He scoffs, unconvinced.

Taking the tray of vegetables out of the oven, my hands shake as I put them on the table with the chicken. I pour two glasses of wine and motion for Aaron to sit.

'Cheers, babe,' I say, sounding far more cheerful than I feel.

He grunts and takes a long swig of his wine. He picks up some serving tongs and starts inspecting the meal.

'Chicken?'

'I hope that's okay. We didn't have anything else, and Mia was asleep. A roast chook from the grocer was the easiest option.'

'Of course you took the easy option.' He loads up his plate and stands up. 'I'm eating this outside.'

Tears streak my face as I pick at a few pieces of chicken before cleaning my plate. I tidy up the rest of the kitchen, go to bed and wait for my punishment.

So much for date night.

Chapter 5

Marnie

Jasper stirs in the bassinet next to our bed. I try not to move, silently wishing he'll go back to sleep. Give us just five more minutes rest. His cries get louder and I sigh. There's something about his first cries in the morning that immediately put me on edge. Is it a sign of the day ahead? What will he cry about later? Fortune telling—a habit the psychologist tells me to cut out.

'Okay, buddy. I get it, you're up.'

I lift him out of his bassinet and onto my chest. He desperately headbutts me a few times before latching on and settling in my arms, relieving my full breasts.

'How did he go last night?' Rob rolls over to face me. I honestly don't know how he sleeps through so many of Jasper's feeds. I sit there in bed, Jasper on my boob, eyes falling out of my head and plotting Rob's death as he snores away peacefully. And it's not exactly a silent exercise. Jasper makes feeding time at the zoo seem civilised with the amount of grunting and snorting he does.

'Five hours since the last feed.' I press tenderly at my breasts—full and sore now, but I'm not complaining about that long stint.

Rob smiles and strokes Jasper's head as he guzzles his breakfast.

'How was your cricket thing last night?'

He props himself up onto an elbow. 'Oh, you know, awkward. It's hard joining a new team, but the guys seem nice and everyone at the club was friendly. I stayed for a few drinks after training. Hope I didn't wake you.'

'Nope,' I lie. I barely sleep these days. I heard him stumble in late. 'What time do you start work again?'

'Eleven this morning. So I'll be home late tonight, and then I have my first match tomorrow.' He looks at me sheepishly, waiting for me to be upset, but I'm too tired to complain.

Rob played cricket when we used to live in the city. The full Saturdays out of the house didn't bother me back then. I'd do my own thing, go for a jog, get my nails done, catch up with friends. But now we're in a new town with a new baby, I'm dreading Saturdays. But I couldn't say, 'No, you can't play'.

'Let me take you and Jasper out for breakfast.'

I can tell he's trying to soften the blow of being out today, tonight, tomorrow and probably tomorrow night, too. Cricket clubs always seem to have post-match functions.

I shrug. 'That's okay. You rest before work.'

Rob's a cop. He got promoted to sergeant recently, which is why we moved from the city. He works long hours. Between his night shifts and Jasper's complete lack of day versus night awareness, he's exhausted. His dark hair is becoming increasingly specked with grey and his green eyes, the eyes I instantly fell in love with all those years ago, now have permanent dark bags below them. But it takes nothing away from how attractive he is. He may be the cricketer, but I'm the one batting above my average.

'Besides, it looks like this little guy has decided to sleep in after all,' I add.

Rob leans over to see for himself. Jasper is sound asleep on my chest.

'Do we call the bomb squad?' Rob whispers.

I hold back a laugh, scared to wake him. When Jasper falls asleep in our arms and we want to move him to his bassinet, we joke about calling the bomb squad because it's such a delicate task. One wrong move and Jasper will explode...into tears. I carefully place him back in his bed and go into the bathroom. I turn on the shower.

'Room for one more?' Rob pokes his head in.

'Nah, I just need a quick refresh before he wakes again.'

Rob looks down, shoulders slumped. 'Okay, I'll go make some coffees.'

I feel bad. Rob and I have barely touched each other since I fell pregnant. It started off as me worrying that we could hurt the baby, despite being reassured that wouldn't happen. Now I don't even know what my excuse is. I feel gross. I don't feel myself at all and I keep pushing Rob away. I've seen the looks we get in the street. He's fit and a few years younger than me. Years of IVF and exhausting fertility treatments took their toll on me, and I look the way I feel—old and run-down. Rob tells me I'm beautiful and that I'm imagining the looks people give. But I know he enjoys the attention.

Jasper's cries filter into the bathroom. I put my head directly under the running water so that it flows into my ears and blocks out the sound. How long can I stay like this?

'He's ready for round two,' Rob calls out. *Dammit.*

I throw on yesterday's clothes with a fresh bra and undies. I take Jasper over to the couch and Rob brings me a coffee. *Bless him.*

'When he's done, we're going for breakfast. I'm not asking, we're going. Let me take a quick shower.'

The shower rumbles through the wall and I look down at Jasper.

'We're lucky to have him, you know?' *I wish I didn't keep pushing him away.*

***

When I'm with Rob, leaving the house doesn't seem daunting. I don't get the same panic about not being able to settle Jasper or forgetting something. We strap Jasper into the pram and walk down to the strip of shops at the end of our street. There's a decent cafe there. We don't go out to eat often, but I've definitely enjoyed their take away coffee on more than one occasion. Lakesfield is a small coastal town about an hour out of Melbourne. We live on the quieter side of the parklands. We have a few shops and cafes on this side, but most of the life in this town is on the other side of the park. There are more restaurants, shops, the cricket, football and netball clubs and the community centre. When I think about shopping on Chapel Street or eating out in one of the hundreds of restaurants scattered amongst the narrow laneways in the city, my stomach turns. I miss the hustle and bustle of Melbourne, but Rob has his dream job here, and Lakesfield is quite beautiful.

Rob pushes the pram with one hand and tries to hold my hand with the other. I let him for a second before grabbing my phone from my pocket and pretending to do something.

He sighs but says nothing.

The cafe is packed for a Friday morning.

'It's too busy, Rob,' I say, 'The noise will bother Jasper.' My heart rate rises. The thought of Jasper becoming unsettled is enough to set me off.

'We can't....' Rob stops himself and runs a hand through his hair. 'Sure, we'll get take away.' I know what he was going to say. *We can't let Jasper dictate everything we do.* But he's not the one who loses so much sleep if we don't.

We take our coffees and bacon and egg rolls to go and find an empty bench at the park to have our breakfast. It's a busy morning in the park. Despite it being a weekday, there are plenty of people around. There's a track that loops around the entire park, including the lake. The lake and the ocean are like bookends for the park. It's a popular route for runners, cyclists and parents pushing prams. One woman looks to be pushing the Starship Enterprise with a baby in a bassinet, a toddler in a seat below and another older child standing on a skateboard connected at the back. It must be heavy. I wonder if I'll ever need a double pram, let alone a triple contraption like that. Something Rob and I should discuss, but we sit on the bench and, as usual, talk about nothing important—Rob's cricket training, my mothers' group, Jasper's catnapping. We don't discuss the things we need to talk about, like my health and how it's affecting our marriage and our fizzling sex-life.

'Marnie! Hey!'

Fleur wheels her pram up to us. She's in activewear today. No gorgeous wraparound dress, but she still looks stunning. Her hair is tied in a loose ponytail, so blonde curls frame her face, and she wears giant sunglasses. Mia is sound asleep in her bassinet.

'Fleur, hi. How are you?'

'Good. I've done a lap of the strip. Are you guys on this side of town, too?' She looks at Rob and smiles.

'Oh, sorry. Fleur, this is my husband, Rob. Rob, this is Fleur. We met at mothers' group yesterday. Yeah, we live down the road.'

Fleur claps her hands. 'Yay, we're basically neighbours. Well, kind of.' She looks down for a moment. 'I live further out. I thought every-one would be from the main side of town. We can totally be walking buddies.'

There's an awkward silence.

'That sounds great,' Rob says, and I hold back from kicking him. 'Don't you reckon, hun?'

'Mmm. Sounds good.'

Fleur digs her phone out of her pocket. 'What's your number? I'll text you to meet up.'

We exchange numbers before Fleur hugs me—twice in two days. This girl is intense. And now we're apparently best friends, sorry 'walking buddies'. *Thanks Rob.*

'Well, she seems nice,' Rob says after Fleur leaves.

I laugh. She must be at least ten years younger than me and have more energy than any amount of coffee could give me. 'She's a bit much. Thanks for throwing me under the bus.'

'Hey, you never know. You might get along well once you give her a chance.'

Classic Rob and his nice guy attitude to everything. I roll my eyes. I wish I were more like him. He probably wishes I was more like Fleur.

Chapter 6

Peyton

When I told Mum that I'd run into Bree at the club and that she wanted to hang out tonight, Mum was more than happy to look after Lucas.

'Oh, such a lovely family. How is Bree?'

'Well, we didn't have time to catch up, but she seems good.' I pretend to care.

'You go get ready. I'm so pleased you're making an effort, finally.' The 'finally' is a typical jab.

I don't mention the hot new guy at the club, the real reason I'm making an effort.

I curl my hair into long, red waves and put my make-up on, pumping milk as I go once again. There's not enough concealer in the world to hide the bags under my eyes from the long nights with Lucas. But they age me a little, and I don't particularly want to look nineteen tonight.

I rummage through my wardrobe. It must be the most unusual teen wardrobe. Half made up of tiny outfits for going out and the other half feeding tops and maternity clothing that I still haven't packed away. I know I have fluoro in here somewhere from someone's fluoro-themed eighteenth birthday party that I can recycle. In the corner of my wardrobe, hard to miss, is the bright pink strapless crop. Paired with my white leather mini skirt and some fluoro pink leg warmers, it makes the perfect outfit for tonight. Fun, but still hot. Nineteen-year-old Peyton stares back at me in the mirror, and my heart aches for her. This is what I should be doing every weekend. I should be losing sleep because I'm doing shots at a bar and cutting up the dance floor, even if the Lakesfield night life is lame. Not losing sleep because my baby is crying for food or cuddles or the umpteenth nappy change.

I deliver the milk to Mum in the lounge. She raises her eyebrows disapprovingly as I enter.

'What? It's a theme night.' I try to justify my outfit, or lack thereof.

She nods and says nothing. But her face says, *'I can't believe you're going out in that. Grow up.'*

I give Lucas a kiss and head out.

'Don't be late,' Mum calls, and I close the door behind me in response. When Lucas is older, I won't be that naggy. I wonder if Mum said that about my nana too.

The cricket club is decorated to suit the theme with lots of bright colours. Inside they've turned most of the lights off and have a black light, which makes my skirt glow. I've been coming here my whole life and the guys who play and hang out here I've known forever. Nothing would ever happen with any of them, but they do still give me the up and down look when I walk in. *They're only human.* And I enjoy the attention. Everyone seems to have dressed for the theme, some more enthusiastically than others. A few of the guys simply sport a glow stick or two around their wrists, while some of the more daring have fluoro leotards and one guy even wears a Borat-style mankini. Certainly not much left to the imagination there. I shudder. Middle-aged men should not be allowed to wear that, although I wouldn't mind seeing a little more skin from the new guy.

Everyone gets a fluoro blue cocktail included in their ticket price, and one of the casual bar staff hands me mine at the door. It tastes like sugar and medicine—gross. And I don't want to stain my teeth with this crap, so I leave mine on a table and head to the bar.

'Cider thanks, Jake.'

Jake has been working behind the bar at the club for as long as I can remember. He's in his late twenties and suffered a severe leg injury from a car accident ten years ago. His focus switched from on-field cricket duties to off-field, and he's manned the bar ever since. He's a friend of my brother and we've always gotten along well. Plus, he's been sneaking me drinks since I was sixteen. *Legend.*

He pours a bottle of cider over some ice in a tall glass.

'Good to see you back out again, Peyt.'

'Good to be back,' I smile. There's only one thing on my mind though. 'Hey, who's the new guy around here?'

'The old guy?'

He wasn't that old, was he? I placed him in his thirties, maybe forties. Either way, he was a babe. I shrug.

'That's Rob. Cop from the city who moved to town recently. He played well today. Already popular with the guys...and girls, I take it.'

I roll my eyes and lift my drink. 'Cheers.'

I take my drink outside, away from the black light that highlights my tiny skirt. There'll be plenty of time to show it off later when the music starts and people get loose on the dancefloor. I scan the crowd for a group I'm happy to silently join, but Bree spots me first. 'You made it!' she squeals.

She has one of the foul blue drinks in her hand. Her short, fluoro green bodycon dress has thin straps and a low cut, revealing some impressive cleavage clearly pushed up by a decent bra. Her dark hair is pulled tightly from her made up face into a high bun that she's poked glow sticks into. Ugh, lame. She almost impressed me with this new look.

'Gotta support the club, right?' and I hold up my drink to cheers her.

We find an empty tall table nearby and take a seat. Need to pace myself on my feet in these shoes, white ankle boots with massive heels. And from the look of relief on Bree's face when she sits, she's happy to be getting off her black, strappy heels too.

'So, how are you? How's Lucas?'

Do I have to talk about Lucas? This is the one place I can pretend to be my old self, with no responsibilities.

'I've seen some pics on Insta, so cute,' she continues.

Dammit. I forgot about my Instagram page and all my posts about Lucas. When he was born, I set it to private and thankfully, none of the guys here follow me. I hope Bree doesn't go telling the world I'm a teen mum. I offer my most convincing smile. 'Thanks, he's good.'

What else do I say to another teenager who knows nothing about motherhood? Um, I'm good despite my nipples being cracked and bloody and my vagina only recently returning to slightly near normal. Oh, and loving the no sleep thing. The bags under my eyes are exactly the look I was hoping for. She doesn't need to hear that. She wouldn't understand that. 'We're good,' I add. 'How've you been?'

This conversation is already so forced and awkward. Small talk like this is why I keep to myself and watch everyone else. Clearly Bree doesn't sense the awkwardness because she waffles on for fifteen minutes about deciding to quit law after one semester and travelling to South America for three months. She's back in town to save over summer and do another big trip to Europe next year.

'Hashtag-living-the-dream,' she says.

I'm going to need more drinks if I have to listen to any more of this.

'I'm going to the bar. Want anything?'

Bree looks at her near full glass of blue poison, 'No thanks. I'll catch you back out here.'

I scan the crowd on my way to the bar. No sign of the hot older guy, but another familiar face takes me by surprise.

'Amalia?'

The quiet woman from mothers' group who didn't share turns to me and smiles. Her long, dark hair frames her face. She's much shorter than me, my boots making the height difference even greater. Her black skinny leg jeans are so Gen Y and she has paired them with a flowy fluorescent yellow top.

'Peyton, right? Sorry, mum brain.'

'Yeah, that's right. I haven't seen you here at the club before.'

She takes in my whole look now, like she's just properly noticing me. One hand fidgets nervously at her long top while the other holds her wine. She takes a big sip. 'I don't come often. Just when my friend drags me down. Does your partner play here?'

I let out a laugh. 'Nope, no partner. I'm a single mum.' I wait for the look of judgement, but it doesn't come. 'My brother used to play here and I still come down a lot. Gotta find something to do on a Saturday night, right? Fluoro fun it is.'

Amalia looks down at her outfit. 'Yeah, I was grateful I had this old thing in the wardrobe. Covers the mum tum well. Although it reminds me of being in my twenties.' She laughs and her cheeks flush.

I wonder how old Amalia is. She doesn't look a heap older than me, but she's at least thirty. Could I be friends with a thirty-year-old? I suppose I've been perving on one and hoping to bump into him, but that's different. Maybe now I have a kid, I'm destined (or doomed) to hang out with an older crowd. I did like the fact she didn't flinch when I said I was a single mum. I glance at her left hand, no ring. Although, that means nothing these days. But maybe she is too.

I lift my empty glass. 'Anyway, I'm off to the bar. See you around, yeah?'

Amalia smiles and nods before turning back to her friends.

I grab another cider and head back outside. I'm reading a text from Mum at the same time. Apparently, Lucas went down to sleep fine. *Of course he did.* That boy bloody loves his grandma.

I look up a moment too late, crashing straight into a wall of man. His chest and stomach are hard and muscular, and his fluoro Hawaiian shirt is now soaked in my cider.

It's him. *Shit.*

'Oh my gosh, I'm so sorry.' I pat at his wet shirt, achieving nothing, before realising how awkward it is that I'm randomly touching him. It doesn't slip by me that his chest and abs feel like a small mountain range under his shirt.

He smiles. 'We really need to stop bumping into each other like this.'

Cringe! What a lame line. But damn, he's hot when he smiles like that. I fake a laugh. 'Yeah. I should watch where I'm going. Your shirt, I'm sorry.'

He looks down at the mess. 'This shirt is disgusting. You've given me a good excuse to go throw on something else. I've got a spare shirt in my cricket bag. But first, I need to replace that drink of yours.'

'No, no. I owe you a drink,' I say, my tone turning flirtatious.

'Even if you hadn't spilled a whole drink on me, I'd want to buy you another.' He looks me up and down now and my whole body warms with excitement.

I grab his hand, suddenly confident. 'To the bar then.'

While we wait in line, he introduces himself. 'I'm Rob, by the way. I'm new to the club.'

'Thought you must be. I'm Peyton. Part of the furniture here.' Kind of a lie since I only started coming back to the club recently, but it sounds cool in my head.

We order our drinks and then Rob goes out to his car to get changed. I wander back outside, hoping to avoid Bree but fail.

'There you are!' Bree drags me over to a table where a bunch of players are sitting.

I do my standard nod hello to the guys without saying much. They talk about today's match and who played well. Rob's name is dropped a few times, and I hope my face doesn't give away the thoughts I'm having right now about him getting changed in the carpark.

'Speak of the devil,' one guy says.

I look up, and there's Rob in a clean, white button-up shirt. Damn, he looks hot.

'What happened to that hideous Hawaiian number you had on?' the same guy asks.

'Just a little drink mishap,' he looks at me, eyes burning into mine.

'For the best I reckon,' another guy says, and the table laughs.

Rob still looks at me and my cheeks burn. I stare back, my tongue playing with the straw in my drink, and for a second I forget there are other people around. Rob takes a big swig of his own drink and looks away. I feel a sense of victory.

More than an hour passes. The guys buy us drinks, and Bree and I never leave the table. Eventually, my bladder gets the better of me. When I stand, I realise how drunk I've gotten. Shit, this is going to hurt tomorrow.

On my way back from the bathroom, I run into Amalia on the dance floor, and I can't help myself. She doesn't invite me into her little circle, but I join them anyway. Everyone's too drunk to notice. Amalia isn't drunk though. She's not swaying on her feet like an inflatable caryard man like the rest of us.

'I'm gonna pay for this tomorrow, aren't I?' I yell out to her over the music.

She smiles. 'Afraid so.'

'Why are you so sober?'

'Have to feed Lila in a few hours.'

Ugh. Responsible parent.

'Oh yeah. I should slow down myself.' For a moment, I attempt to count the drinks I've had and the hours that have passed and calculate when I can feed Lucas. Then I shake it off. I've got formula. Whatever.

'So, is Lila's dad here with you?' I change the subject.

'Not sure where he is.' She glances around. 'I'm going to the ladies.'

Amalia rushes off, and I'm unsure how to take her answer. Does she not know where he is at the club or tonight or at all? Seems a strange response.

Bree and the guys join us on the dance floor. It's now packed. The black light makes everyone's teeth glow and the guys with white sneakers are trying out dance moves with extra kicks, fascinated by their own feet. I lose myself in the music, a mix of noughties classics and some newer stuff.

Rob comes up behind me and starts to dance. He isn't touching me, but I can feel his breath every so often on my neck. I turn to face him, and we keep dancing, not touching despite the temptation and roaring heat in my belly. I still don't know how old he is, but he dances like my dad. He looks goofy and is trying to sing along to songs he clearly doesn't know well, if at all. His moves are a bit of a turn off, but the way his eyes bore into mine while we dance and the way his arm muscles flex from his dancing make me care less that he's no Magic Mike.

He leans in and my breath catches in my throat. 'Come outside.'

It's getting hot on the dance floor, both the crowded space and the company, so I follow him out. The deck is basically empty now, with most people taking advantage of the DJ. There are a few smokers up one end. Rob and I go down the other end.

I lean back against the rail with the oval behind me. My hands grip the rail on either side of my body. Rob has a hand near one of mine and he's turned side on to face me. I lean my head back and look up at the stars. The movement pushes my chest out and hitches my already short crop top further up my torso. The breeze cools more of my exposed skin. Skin that doesn't go unnoticed by Rob, who lets out an audible breath.

'Only you could make fluoro look this...'

I look back at him, my red waves falling to frame my face. He doesn't finish his sentence. Just shakes his head. He lifts his hand to my face and tucks a stray curl behind my ear.

Heat pools in my stomach, and I let out a sigh at his touch. He stares at my lips, and I instinctively run my tongue across my upper lip. He takes that as an invitation and moves in closer. Then his lips are on mine, and my first thought is how drunk I feel and the taste of my cider mixing with his beer doesn't help. But the feeling passes, and I relax, opening my mouth to let his tongue in. He doesn't hesitate, pushing himself up against me and the rail. I run my hands down his solid front, feeling the outlines of his muscles. It makes him groan and kiss me harder. My back is pressed firmly against the rail behind me and I use it as leverage to get closer to him, feeling myself losing control.

He pulls away, breathing heavily and gripping the rail on either side of my hips.

'Sorry,' he says, still out of breath.

I run a finger down the front of his shirt, letting it continue to below where his shirt ends. He closes his eyes and exhales loudly.

'Don't be,' I say.

His phone buzzes, and I'm annoyed when he checks it. 'Shit, I've gotta go.'

I roll my eyes. Leave a girl hanging, dammit.

He hands me a card. Sergeant Robert Jones. Even his job makes him sound old. 'My number's on there.' He pecks me on the cheek and leaves.

I give myself a moment to cool down from both that kiss and feeling annoyed and rejected. I head back towards the clubhouse, keen to get home myself now.

'That looked heated.' Amalia is sitting by herself at one of the tall tables near the door. She's got a big coat covering the front of her and I can hear the unmistakable hum of a breast pump. 'Came out to pump, didn't expect a show.' She laughs.

I flush red. 'That's so embarrassing. Did anyone else see?'

'Nope, I came out here for privacy. Your secret's safe with me,' Amalia winks.

I mean, it's not a secret, but the boys would give me so much crap if they'd seen that. 'Thanks. I'm heading off. See you Thursday at mothers' group, yeah?'

Amalia nods, and I head home, praying the hangover gods are kind to me.

Chapter 7

Amalia

I'm outside pumping breastmilk and tapping out a message to Mrs Casci.

Be home soon.

The three dots indicate that she's replying but she's notoriously slow on the texts. Who can blame her though? She's seventy-two.

No worries, pet. Take your time. Love Nonna.

She insists Lila and I call her Nonna. Mrs Casci is my elderly neighbour who looks after Lila every Thursday evening and some Saturdays too. Her grandchildren live interstate, so Lila is a pleasant distraction from how desperately she misses them.

Despite her message, I want to get out of here. I'm no longer in the mood. I can't believe Peyton was at the club tonight. Mothers' group on Thursday had not gone well for me. I lost all my nerve in there and didn't say a word. Then Peyton asked me about myself tonight, and I basically froze again. I'm supposed to be bonding with these women. I'm meant to be finding that person who will make motherhood the beautiful experience my mum had. Instead I'm bordering between painfully shy and outright rude.

My friend Kya, basically my only friend, dragged me to the club again tonight. I'd never seen Peyton here before, and I was somewhat of a regular recently. She strutted around in her mini skirt and crop top like she owned the place, but to be fair, everyone seemed to know her and love her. I couldn't believe how hot she looked. Like, come on. You have a baby! You shouldn't look like that. But nevertheless, she was a sweetheart, and I should applaud her courage to have a baby at her age. I don't think she could be more than twenty, if that.

***

When I get home Mrs Casci makes me a cup of tea. She really is an angel. 'She went down like a dream,' she says as I sip my tea.

I smile. 'Thank you so much for watching her.'

'It's my pleasure. I love my time with Lila.' Her words are so genuine that a lump forms in my throat that I work hard to swallow. Mrs Casci is the closest thing to a grandparent that Lila has. She's the closest thing to family that either of us has.

I walk her out and she crosses the lawn to her own door. She waves and goes inside. Minutes later, there's a knock at the door. When I open it, my pulse quickens.

'Hey babe,' Marcus says. 'I waited ages for Mrs C to leave. Can I see Lil?'

I stand there frozen. I should say no. Of course I should say no. 'I don't think that's a good idea.'

'She's my daughter too.'

'You should've thought about that before you screwed your personal trainer.'

Marcus' hands clench to fists by his sides. 'I've apologised a thousand times for that. We can make this work.'

We absolutely cannot make this work, I think to myself. My father would've never cheated on my mum. 'No, we can't.'

Marcus and I met a few years ago when he came to the bank I worked at to cancel a credit card. It'd been stolen, and it was hilarious watching him explain that the charges at various unsavoury venues were not him. I'd been laughing so hard my manager had a stern talking with me. Two nights later, we went on our first date. Now I'm a single mum to his daughter because he cheated on me when I was six months pregnant.

Marcus wants a relationship with Lila and me, but he made his choice. He helped decorate the nursery during the day and then snuck off to the gym for late 'training sessions' at night. I'd wanted to kill him. He'd left his phone at home one night and it buzzed on the table near me.

Where are you?

I can't wait to see you.

I'm wearing something special just for you.

I scrolled up through the previous messages. Arrogant jerk didn't even bother to delete them. They'd been going behind my back for months. I lay in bed that night waiting for him to come home thinking about how I could finish him. Poison? I didn't know how to get my hands on any. Smother him in his sleep? I was six months pregnant. I didn't have the strength. Before he got home, I'd come to terms with just kicking him out. After all, I needed his money. He was going to have to pay me child support, and I didn't want to go back to work straight away. I needed that money.

Since I'd ended things, he clearly regretted his decision. But I'd also seen another side to him. He had a shocking temper, and I was scared every time I had to turn him away.

Marcus slams his fist on the brick wall beside the front door.

'She deserves to know her dad,' he says. He no longer appears to be angry. His voice is softer and his shoulders slump. He's sad. But I don't care.

'She's asleep. You need to leave.' I close the door and wait for him to block it or start banging on it once it clicks closed, but he doesn't. Through the peephole, I see him walk back to his car. He looks up at the window to the room where Lila sleeps. The room we decorated together. Such a jerk.

Chapter 8

Fleur

As soon as I hit send on my text to Marnie to catch up for that walk, I regret it. I don't know what I was thinking even suggesting it and then following through with it. I don't know why I do a lot of things. Aaron got home late last night stinking of beer, and I guess I need a reason to get away from the house. It takes so much energy to be the Fleur I want everyone else to see.

While Mia naps, I wash and blow dry my hair and put on a touch of mascara. It's warm outside, but I need to keep my back covered, so I opt for a tight black t-shirt and leopard print leggings. Mia wakes up as I finish putting my sneakers on. I feed her and put her in the pram to meet Marnie down at the park.

I wait about ten minutes before Marnie comes rushing up to us with Jasper in the pram. Her mousy brown hair looks freshly washed and is still dripping, leaving wet patches on her baggy t-shirt. Her leggings are black highlighting the milky spew marks. Rookie error. Or maybe she doesn't care.

'Sorry, I'm late! Had to take advantage of a catnap to shower.' She runs a hand through her soaking hair. 'Clearly the nap didn't last long, and now I'm dripping wet and covered in spew.'

I feel bad for judging her. I can understand how it could happen. But I could never go out looking like that. I'd have to cancel. Plus, if Aaron knew I went out looking in any way dishevelled, I'd cop it.

'Oh, you poor thing. Text me next time if you need to change times or whatever. Mia and I are flexible. It's fine.'

Marnie smiles, but her cheeks flush.

'Should we do a lap of the park then?' I ask.

'Sounds good. Maybe Jasper will finish that nap if I'm lucky.'

I hold up crossed fingers and we walk. 'So where's Rob today?' I ask, remembering her rather handsome husband from the other morning.

Marnie's shoulders noticeably sag, and I worry I've said the wrong thing. 'He's in bed. He had a late night at a cricket function last night and starts night shift tonight.'

'Oh,' I pause. 'It must be so hard to have a baby with a partner doing night shift. What does he do?'

'He's a cop. Recently promoted, which is why we moved out here. It has its perks at times.' Her tone is far from convincing. 'But yeah, night shifts are tough.'

I think about my nights. On one hand, I love seeing Aaron bath Mia but sometimes I wonder if it'd be easier if it were only me and her. 'You're good for giving him the night off last night too.' I'm not even sure why I say this given Aaron wouldn't give a toss if I wanted him home or not.

Marnie lets out a laugh. 'Not sure I had much of a say. But he's new here and I want him to meet people.' She sighs. 'I wish he hadn't stayed out so late. He stunk of alcohol when he stumbled in.'

I know that feeling and that stench too well.

She continues, 'The worst part is, he used to always text me all night when he was out. Last night I heard nothing. When I finally gave in and contacted him, he rushed home. I don't know. It's unlike Rob.'

'Well, that's good that he rushed home though, right?' I say, trying to reassure her. Aaron would never do that for me.

'Mmmm. I've got a weird feeling.'

'Have you guys been together long?'

'Forever.' Marnie stops for a second to tie up her hair. 'Sorry. This wet hair's annoying me. Yeah, we've been married ten years, trying to get pregnant most of the last decade.'

'That must've been so hard for you guys.' I feel guilty about how easy conceiving was for us.

'Yep. And now that we're finally here, and we have Jasper, things are different. It's my fault.'

I stop walking and touch Marnie's arm. She stops too. 'It's not your fault if you're not feeling right after having Jasper. Maybe you should talk to Liz about getting some help.' I wish I could take my own advice.

Marnie's eyes water and she stands there for a moment, saying nothing, hopefully thinking about my suggestion. Then she shakes her head and smiles. 'It's fine. I'm overthinking things. Anyway, tell me about you. Are you married?'

It worries me that she's changed the subject so quickly. I, of all people, know how it feels to hide behind a smile.

'Yeah, married my high school sweetheart.'

'Aww, sweet.'

I laugh because that's literally the same reaction everyone gives. If only they knew the truth.

'His name is Aaron. He's an accountant.'

'So he's at home now?'

'Umm no, he's working,' I lie.

'On a Sunday? That's keen.'

'Living off one wage now, you know what it's like.'

Marnie nods, and I hope she bought it. I don't want to tell her that my gambling, alcoholic, violent husband is actually at the racetrack throwing away what little money we do have and getting drunk.

'Where does he work?'

'At the agency on the main strip.'

Shit. That was too much information for me to share when I'm lying about where he is.

'He sounds dedicated.'

I nod. Dedicated to blowing our money down the drain.

We continue our lap of the park. The conversation is relatively boring after that. We talk about feeding and sleep patterns and pelvic floor exercises, something I've totally neglected.

It's about three pm when we get back to where we started.

'Thanks for the walk, Fleur. I need to rush though if Rob's going to see Jasper before work.'

'No worries, it was nice. See you Thursday.'

When I get home, Aaron isn't back. I lie Mia down on her playmat, and she plays with a soft toy the hospital gave her at birth. I already know what state Aaron will be in when he gets home. From experience, the best thing to do is to have food ready. I put some pasta on the stove and defrost a tub of Bolognese sauce I made and froze last week. I leave everything ready on the bench to be heated again when he or I feel like eating, and I feed Mia. She needs a bath, but I don't dare take that responsibility off Aaron again, even if it makes me nervous when he's drunk.

At five, he stumbles in. The smell of beer and cigarettes is overwhelming, and I worry about poor Mia's little lungs breathing it all in.

'Hey, babe,' I say, smiling. 'How was your day?'

He glares at me. 'Don't ask.' He pokes around at the food on the bench. 'What's this shit?'

'Spag Bol. Thought you'd be hungry when you got back.'

He scrunches up his nose. 'Suddenly lost my appetite.'

My heart sinks. I'm never good enough. He comes over to where Mia and I sit.

'Is she done?' he asks as I finish burping her.

'Yep, finished.'

He snatches her from my arms. 'Hello beautiful girl,' he says in a voice that makes me feel sick with how fake it is. 'Do you need a bath, my baby?'

He sways on his feet, Mia in his hands. 'Is that a good idea?'

His head snaps in my direction. 'What's that supposed to mean?'

I immediately regret saying anything. 'Well, you've had a big day. I can do it if you like.'

'No.' He comes right up to me and leans down so his face is level with mine. The alcohol stench becomes stronger, and I clamp my mouth closed. 'You aren't taking this off me again. I'm capable of bathing my daughter.'

He heads toward the bathroom and I get up to follow. 'Piss off, Fleur. I don't need your supervision.'

I freeze where I am. I know Aaron would never harm Mia but a drunk bathing a baby.... What am I supposed to do?

I decide to do some washing and ironing. The laundry is opposite the bathroom. I'll be able to hear everything but easily pretend I'm doing my own thing.

I sigh with relief as the water gurgles down the plughole and Mia giggles. Aaron takes her to her room and sings to her. I wonder what happened to the man I love. Part of him is in there somewhere still. I can hear that part of him singing our sleepy daughter love songs right now. But that man hasn't seen me in a long time.

The door to Mia's room closes, and I quickly turn back to the ironing board in front of me. Aaron's hand grips my upper arm and spins me to face him.

'Don't think I didn't see what you were doing in here—checking on me.' He's yelling now.

I shake my head. 'Babe, I'm doing the laundry. That's all.'

'Don't lie to me.' His voice is loud, and I'm conscious of the open windows.

'I'm not lying. Aaron, calm down, the neighbours…'

'I don't give a shit about the neighbours!'

Then he lifts the iron and swings to strike my face. I lift my hand in defence and the palm of my hand burns. I scream in pain. Aaron drops the iron and covers my mouth.

'Shut up, Fleur. You don't want to bother those neighbours you're so worried about.'

He shoves me backwards and storms out. I lean against the wall behind me and sink down to the floor, my body trembling. I inspect the damage to my hand. A decent burn to most of my palm, but not anything I can't handle myself. My nursing training has come in handy on more than one occasion. I run the laundry tap. I have to use my good hand to hold the burnt one still under the running water because it won't stop shaking. It stings and tears roll down my cheeks. I can't believe he went for my face. He's never that careless, always aiming for parts of my body that he knows I'll cover with clothes. I stand at the tap for a good twenty minutes, letting the cool water ease the burning sensation in my hand.

I find some antiseptic and dab it on the area. The last thing I need is an infection and having to explain the injury at the hospital. I bandage my hand and head back to the kitchen. I want to eat quickly and go to bed. It's best to avoid any more time with Aaron while he's like this.

He's sitting at the bench eating the food I prepared. I put my bowl of pasta in the microwave.

'This is delicious, thanks hun.' He looks at my bandaged hand, panic in his eyes. 'Are you okay?'

The way he can flip like this, I don't get it. 'Yep, fine.'

'Look, Fleur, I'm sorry. I lost too much at the track today. You know, a mate said it was a sure thing, and the bloody donkey came dead last. I'm stressed. You understand, right?'

I nod, too scared to say or do anything else. The microwave beeps, and I remove my dinner. We eat in silence at the bench.

I'm attempting to wash the dishes one-handed when the doorbell rings. I look at Aaron, confused. He shrugs but doesn't move from where he has now slumped on the couch. So much for being sorry. He won't help with the dishes when I'm clearly struggling and now won't get off his ass to answer the door.

I open the door, and a familiar face greets me.

'Hi ma'am, I'm Sergeant Jones. We had a report of raised voices and screams earlier tonight.' Recognition dawns on the man's face. 'Fleur?'

I nod, my eyes wide, terrified of what Aaron's going to do. Plus, I can't imagine how hideous I look right now. I'm not wearing makeup, and my eyes are probably puffy from crying. What will he tell Marnie?

'Fleur, it's Rob, Marnie's husband.'

I smile, 'Yeah, I remember. Can I help you?'

'Who is it?' Aaron yells from the couch.

I turn to him nervously, but I'm eager to play my part, otherwise I'll be punished. My voice is upbeat. 'Babe, it's the cops.'

Aaron jumps to his feet and races over. 'Hey mate. What can we do for you?'

Rob repeats himself. 'We had a report of a disturbance here earlier tonight. Do you know anything about this?'

Aaron scratches his head. 'No, mate.' He puts his arm around me. 'We've been home all night, just finished dinner.'

I smile and lift my hand to Aaron's at my shoulder. Rob notices the bandage.

'Fleur, what happened to your hand?'

Aaron looks at me, eyes narrowing. 'Um, do you two know each other?'

'Rob is married to one of the mums in mothers' group.' My voice shakes. 'I met him the other day at the park.'

I feel Aaron's body tense next to mine. I'm going to pay for this.

'Your hand?' Rob presses.

'Oh, ironing accident. I'm sure you know how it is, getting distracted by a newborn at home.' I laugh, hoping he buys the story.

Rob pauses, eyeing us closely. 'Look, here's my card. Let me know if you guys think of anything or hear anything yourselves.'

Aaron snatches the card before I can take it. 'Will do,' he says before closing the door. He watches as Rob walks back down the driveway and hops into his car. He pulls me in close, squeezing my burnt hand. 'Making friends with cops now? Be careful, Fleur.'

His voice is cold and my eyes water from the fresh wave of pain in my hand. Then he goes back to the couch.

I take myself to bed and lie there crying. *What do I do? How do I get out of this mess?*

Chapter 9

Marnie

Jasper wakes for the hundredth time since I put him to bed last night. I guess the long stint he gave me the other night was a tease. Sunlight sneaks through the gaps in the blinds and I call it—time to get up. Rob was at work all night. It's like Jasper knew I was on my own, easier to defeat. And boy do I feel defeated today.

As I lift him from the bassinet, I look into his big green eyes, like his daddy's. Lowering him to my chest, I help him find his breakfast, and then I let the tears fall. I'm so tired, and I feel so alone. I massively overshared with Fleur yesterday, don't know what I was thinking. But Rob is acting weird, and I can hardly blame him. I'm always sobbing. I'm never dressed in anything besides spew-stained activewear, and I haven't let him touch me for the better part of a year. I see myself in the mirror and I don't recognise myself anymore. And yet Rob is the same successful, kind, fit guy I met over a decade ago.

The front door slams shut. What timing. He's home, and I'm crying yet again. I wipe the tears and close my eyes. I pretend to sleep, hoping my red eyes pass for tiredness.

'Marnie,' Rob whispers and shakes my leg.

I blink my eyes a few times. 'Sorry, must've fallen asleep, long night.'

He tilts his head at me. Lying to a cop is so pointless.

'Marns, you need to stay awake when you're holding Jasper. Here...' he holds his hands out. 'Want me to take him, and you can rest?'

Yes. 'Nah, he's feeding. Best leave him.'

'Okay, well, I'll take a shower, then make some coffee.'

A sad smile crosses my lips. *He's too good for me.*

***

Jasper goes back to sleep. Typical that he's sleeping more than thirty minutes at a time now that Rob is home. I sit on a stool at the bench and rest my head in my hands.

'Don't you need to go to bed? You've got night shift again later,' I say to Rob, who's pottering around the kitchen. The kitchen is beautiful. It's one of the main reasons we bought the house. It's modern, with shiny new appliances and plenty of space. The mosaic tile splashback is like something out of a home reno show, and the marble bench is stunning. We certainly couldn't have afforded something like this in Melbourne. You get much more bang for your buck outside of the city.

'Breakfast first,' he says and starts buttering me some toast. 'Vegemite or peanut butter?'

'Vegemite please.'

Rob's mostly helpful, but making me breakfast between night shifts, that's unusual. He's usually keen to get his sleep.

'How was Saturday night at the cricket club?' I ask, still feeling annoyed at how drunk and late he came home.

He avoids eye contact. 'Yeah, good. Good to meet the guys properly.'

'Big night?'

'Mmm, probably a little too big. Sorry I was home late.' He glances up at me.

I stare at my toast. 'You and Jasper are both party animals it seems.'

'Tonight is my last night shift, then I'll do the night feeds for a few days. You can get some sleep.'

I smile. 'Thanks, sounds great.' It really does.

We eat our toast in silence. I sneak a few glances at Rob. His face is covered in stubble and the bags under his eyes look darker. I suppose that's what a big night out followed by night shift does, or maybe it's parenthood. But there's more to his look than just fatigue.

'Everything okay?' I ask.

Rob plays with the crusts of his toast, then sighs. 'Not really.'

My stomach flips. He's done something wrong. He got drunk and did something stupid. I shouldn't have asked. I count my breaths, preparing for the worst.

'I shouldn't be saying anything. But I'm worried about your friend Fleur.'

I spit out a mouthful of coffee. 'What!?' I wasn't expecting that. Rob met Fleur for all of two minutes at the park. Why is he worried about her?

'I got a call out to her house last night. Raised voices and screaming.'

I sit up straighter. 'Oh. And...'

'Well, when I got there, her and her husband said everything was fine. But Fleur had a bandaged hand, and I got a bad vibe from the guy.'

'Did you say she had a bandaged hand?'

Rob nods.

'That's weird. I saw her in the afternoon and her hands were fine.'

He rubs at the stubble around his chin. 'Ironing accident, she said. Not sure if I buy it.'

'I should go over there and see if she's okay.'

Rob stands abruptly. 'No, absolutely not. I don't want you going to that house. And you can't ask her about it. I shouldn't be telling you about work. It's inappropriate.'

I exhale loudly. This puts me in such a difficult position. How am I supposed to pretend I don't know?

He sits back down. 'Maybe if she has the bandage on when you see her next, you can ask. But otherwise, say nothing.'

'Mmm.'

'Marnie, I'm serious. Do you understand? This is my job we're talking about.'

'Yep, I won't say anything. So what are you doing about it?'

He sighs. 'Nothing. I've been worrying about her all night. But there's not much I can do at this stage.'

I shake my head. We always argue about law enforcement and all the hoops cops have to jump through. We're always on the same side, but I get annoyed that Rob never takes a stand. It's not his fault though. I lean over to him and take his hand. I know how much this must be bothering him now.

That's probably why he's being so nice this morning. If he can't help Fleur, he'll go over the top to help me instead.

Chapter 10

Peyton

It's been a long week. I was so hungover on Sunday. A baby plus a hangover is some kind of cruel torture, and Mum was only too keen to make me suffer more. But I couldn't help but feel floaty after my night with Rob. Things had gotten heated, in a good way. I'd messaged him all throughout Sunday, and he had responded with flirty texts back and forth. But then Monday rolled around, and it's been total silence ever since. I'm not desperate; two unreturned texts and I'm done. I won't keep trying, but I can't say I'm not a bit disappointed. Some playful texting is fun, but whatever, his loss.

The rest of the week was newborn monotony. Eat, play, sleep, repeat.

This morning is session two of mothers' group and despite finding it lame last week, I'm looking forward to it. It's something to break up the day, plus I wouldn't mind chatting to Amalia again. She seemed cool on Saturday night and maybe she knows Rob, not that I care or anything.

I decide to walk to the community centre today. The weather is nice, and Lucas hates the car lately. I braided my hair this morning and it hangs over one shoulder. I figure a braid will give me some nice waves for when I go to the cricket club tonight. Not that I'm trying hard or anything.

I arrive at the centre, and Fleur is standing outside. She's fumbling around in her nappy bag, looking for something. She takes out a little compact and starts brushing its contents over her eyes.

'Hey, you okay?' I ask.

She startles, quickly pulling her sunglasses down over her eyes and looks up at me. 'Yeah, of course. Just a little touch up. Sweated half of it off already.' Her voice is still upbeat like last week, but there's a shakiness to it.

Her sunglasses cover most of her face and her long sleeve dress is at odds with today's weather. Then I spy a bandage poking out from one sleeve and wrapping around her hand.

She sees me staring. 'Don't mix ironing with sleep deprivation.' She laughs, holding up her hand.

I force a laugh in response. I can't comment because Mum does my ironing.

'I'll see you in there,' I say and head into the centre. When I turn back, her glasses are back on her head and she's continuing her touch up. Not sure why she bothers. No one else seemed to make an effort with their appearance last week. Well, besides Hanbi with her corporate chic look but I don't think that was for us.

Everyone else is already inside. There are two empty spots in the circle. One on either side of the facilitator, Liz. Everyone's avoiding sitting next to her, knowing she made people share going around the circle, starting from either side of her. No one wants to be the first to share. One of the spare seats has Marnie on the other side of it, the older mum. *No thanks.* The other spare seat's neighbour is Amalia. I take that one.

'Hey,' I whisper to her.

She nods in response but says nothing. Kind of rude.

'How'd you pull up after Saturday?'

Amalia's eyes dart around the room. 'Yeah, fine,' she whispers. 'You?'

'Do *not* let me drink like that again,' I say dramatically. 'Lucas was ten times more painful with a hangover.'

She smiles as Fleur comes in and takes the last seat next to Marnie.

Liz gets started. 'Welcome to your second session. This week we will discuss relationships.'

Ugh. Really?

'I acknowledge that not every child's born into a home with a mum and dad. There are single parents, same-sex parents, the list goes on. But each of you deserves someone in your life that can offer support to you and your child.'

I glance around the room. The other mums are nodding along, except for Fleur. She's staring down at Mia in her arms, avoiding eye contact with anyone.

'Today we're going to share who our support person is and hopefully I can provide you with additional avenues of support as well. Of course, this is optional. You don't have to share anything.'

Not wanting to go first, I keep my eyes looking straight ahead. I don't want to turn to the side and meet Liz's gaze. I'm not ashamed to be a single mum, but I don't want to start.

'Peyton, how about you get us started?'

Dammit.

I consider passing and saying nothing, but I'm not ashamed. I need to suck it up and own it.

I smile. 'Sure. Well, I'm a single mum.' I pause to see who judges me. A few sympathetic nods are all I get. 'I live at home with my mum and dad. Mum is definitely my biggest support. She looks after Lucas a lot. He adores her.'

'And any support from Lucas' father?'

Surely that's inappropriate to ask.

Last I'd heard, Lucas' dad was living it up in Sydney doing some sports related university degree. I tried to call him when Lucas was born, but he'd blocked my number. It's sad, really, because we were good mates who drank too much one night. Mum told his parents about the situation, mainly because she thought they might want to know their grandson. We didn't want anything from them. But they denied that it was their son's child. They wanted nothing getting in the way of his future, I guess.

I shake my head. There's an awkward pause, and Liz moves on to asking Amalia.

Everyone looks at Amalia, who says nothing.

Another awkward silence, and I wonder if Liz regrets starting this discussion.

'You don't have to share, that's fine.'

Zara, the woman who annoyed me last week, is next. What self-admiring B.S. is she going to spin this week to make half of us feel like crap?

'It's me and hubby, Joe, at home. Been married for three years. He's my soulmate. Little Tiana looks like her daddy.'

'Beautiful and what support does he offer you with Tiana—bottles, bath time?'

'Oh no, definitely not. T is exclusively breastfed.'

How could we forget?

'And I bath her before my husband gets home, but he'll play with Tiana on the weekend. He also reads her a bedtime story before she falls asleep in our bed.'

Liz nods and smiles. I roll my eyes, and Hanbi stifles a laugh.

Hanbi is next. She's, once again, dressed for an office and I truly wonder if she's come straight from work.

'My husband is a stay-at-home dad. He does it all. I work full time.'

Zara gasps, and Hanbi shoots her a glare that makes me flinch. I guess I was right.

'My career has always been important to me, but my husband wanted kids, and so this is the arrangement that works for us.'

'But how do you feed umm...' Zara stumbles over the baby's name.

'Sienna? I breastfeed before and after work, and she has formula during the day.'

'Oh,' Zara doesn't hide the judgement in her voice.

'Sounds like you have a supportive husband,' Liz says, trying to ease the tension. 'How lovely for Sienna to have her dad at home all the time.'

Hanbi gives Liz a grateful smile. Although I don't think she cares at all what Zara thinks of her, and I admire her story. Breaking the stereotype. I like it.

Then Liz adds, 'Will he be joining us for any sessions? He's more than welcome as Sienna's primary caregiver?'

'No, he's shy. Plus, he thinks it's important for me to meet some other women with children. I don't have any mum friends.'

I offer her a smile. I feel you!

Marnie is next.

'I've been married to my husband for ten years. He's great with Jasper, does some feeds overnight and because he works different shifts, he gets to play with him often during the day.'

Boring.

'And Fleur, how about you?' Liz asks the last mum in the group.

Fleur looks up and smiles brightly. 'I married my high school sweetheart, Aaron.'

The other mums smile. I try not to gag.

'He loves Mia. Bath time is their absolute favourite time of day together, and it's adorable to watch.'

I don't know how someone can speak with this much positivity and energy all the time. It's sickening.

'And besides bath time, is he supportive of you?'

Fleur's eyes flash with panic. 'Yeah, of course.'

Marnie leans over and pats Fleur's leg. She shoots Marnie a warning glare and moves her leg away.

Liz spends some time explaining how we can get our partners, or parents, or other support people involved in our baby's life more. We go through bath time, songs, massages, and I know this is all going to come far more naturally to my mum with Lucas than it will to me. I suck at this mum gig. Before he was born, I tried to prepare myself. I follow all the Instagram pages of mum bloggers and have some great play ideas for when he's older. But mostly, all I see is kids wearing designer outfits and mum's tagging this brand and that with #ad written at the end of every post.

The last part of the session is free time for us to catch up with each other. We're supposed to be forming friendships that'll extend beyond these group sessions. My mum's nagging voice sounds in my head to make an effort, have some fun and do it for Lucas' sake. The words are out of my mouth before I realise.

'Anyone want to go over to the surf club for a drink?'

Fleur and Marnie are in deep, seemingly heated conversation, which they suddenly stop to look at me. The other mums do the same. *What the hell am I doing?* They're probably judging me for wanting to drink in the middle of the day on a Thursday. Worse still, they're probably judging me for drinking while I'm *supposed* to be breastfeeding. The silence seems to drag on forever.

'I'm keen,' Marnie says, finally.

And then it's like the floodgates open. Fleur, Amalia and Zara are all wanting to join.

'I would kill for a wine right now, but I have to go back to work ladies,' Hanbi says.

I'm disappointed she can't come. I dig her 'take no shit' attitude, and I know I'm going to have to work soon if I am to have any hope of fleeing the nest in the next five years so I'm keen to quiz her on the work-life balance.

'Maybe next week?' I say.

Who am I? This could be an absolute disaster. Why am I making plans with middle aged women?

'So, surf club in ten?' Fleur asks and we all agree.

Chapter 11

Amalia

The Lakesfield Surf Lifesaving Club is a popular spot in town. The coffee is decent, the drinks are reasonably priced, and food is delicious. The place plays host to knock off drinks, kids' birthday parties, casual dinners and, apparently, mothers' groups.

When Peyton suggested we go for a drink, I was relieved. I'd once again said nothing in our mothers' group session and thought perhaps a glass of wine might boost my confidence to connect with these women.

The convoy of prams travels up the ramp to the second floor where the bar and dining room are. We find a spot out on the balcony where we can park the prams without getting in the way of too many people. It's a beautiful day, warm but the breeze off the ocean makes it pleasant. From our table, we can see the waves crashing on the beach. It's Thursday and school is back, so there aren't a lot of people out there, but the red and yellow flags are in position and the lifeguards are on duty.

We all sit. Zara and Marnie are juggling their babies and flicking through drinks menus while Fleur, Peyton and I are the lucky ones this time whose kids fell asleep in their prams on the way over. A young waiter walks out onto the balcony, and Peyton groans, lowering herself in her chair as though she's trying to hide.

'Peyton, hey,' the waiter says.

'Hey.'

He glances at the prams around us and then back at Peyton, be-coming increasingly nervous. 'Um, what can I get you ladies?'

We decide to share a bottle of chardonnay, except for Zara who orders a juice. Apparently alcohol could dry up our breast milk, and she rattles off a bunch of stats while the poor waiter stands there white as a ghost.

'Anything else?' he asks.

No one says anything, and he races off, bumping into one of the prams on his way.

'What was that?' asks Marnie.

Peyton shakes her head and sighs. 'I went to school with him. We're mates, well we were. Then his best friend knocked me up, fled town and now none of the guys speak to me. So yeah, that was awkward.'

There's silence. I want to say something. I want to tell her that I know what it feels like to be let down by the father of your child. I understand the betrayal. Our situations are different, but ultimately we're both single mothers. My nerves get the better of me though, and I say nothing. I don't know why I feel so anxious. Perhaps I've put too much pressure on this group and these women and what they potentially mean to me.

Fleur breaks the silence. 'Men can be such pigs.'

'Didn't you say earlier that you married your high school sweet-heart?' Peyton asks.

Fleur flushes. 'Well yeah. But you know, no one's perfect.' She rubs her hand. It's wrapped in a bandage. I hadn't noticed earlier, and of course I don't ask.

A different waiter comes out with our drinks. He stares at Peyton as she places the bottle of wine in a bucket of ice and sets down four glasses and a juice. No doubt the other guy had begged him to swap tables and offered him some gossip with the trade. Peyton doesn't seem too bothered. The girl is stunning, and as I saw on Saturday, she's having fun.

Marnie opens the bottle and pours us all a big glass. 'Cheers,' she says holding up her glass and a chorus of cheers follows. Including me. The first thing I've said besides agreeing to a bottle of wine.

The first glass of wine goes down easily, and Peyton orders another bottle before anyone can protest. Besides Tiana, who's in Zara's arms feeding, the babies are still sleeping soundly. There is some kind of mothers' group God looking down on us right now.

Before long, everyone is relaxed, and we're chirping away as though we've known each other forever.

'I could've killed my husband last night,' Marnie says, laughing. 'Jasper screamed the house down when I changed his nappy after a feed, and he lay there, sleeping soundly. God help me if there was an intruder or fire alarm and I needed him.'

The other women laugh. Husband talk seems to be a popular topic. Peyton seems to find it amusing, while I find it hard. Ideally, I'd have married Marcus eventually. I should be sitting here contributing my pet hates about him. Not mourning the gap he's left in our lives.

'I'm pretty sure Aaron doesn't even know Mia wakes up overnight. Or that she poops. Or wears clothing that needs washing. Or has dummies that need sterilising.' Fleur rolls her eyes. 'He knows how to bath her, and that is precisely all he knows.'

'You guys ought to say something to your partners,' Zara pipes up. 'I put down expectations soon after Tiana was born.'

It takes all my strength not to roll my eyes. Didn't she say earlier that her husband does a book before bed and some play on the weekend? That doesn't exactly scream *hands-on-dad*.

'So what does he do for you then?' Peyton asks, as though reading my mind.

'Tiana feeds a few times overnight and she finds me in bed when she's ready. Joe will get up and make me a herbal tea. It contains fenugreek, highly recommend it for lactation.'

'He gets up and makes you a tea every night?' Marnie asks.

'Yep,' Zara smiles.

'Wow. I'm grateful if I get a coffee in the morning. And let's face it, the coffee goes stone cold before I ever get to it anyway,' Marnie says.

'What *is* hot coffee?' Fleur says.

We laugh. Well, all of us besides Zara. I'm not sure if it's because she can't relate to our varying levels of at-home support, or if it's because she doesn't drink coffee. Heaven forbid she consumes caffeine while breastfeeding.

'What about you Amalia?' Peyton asks.

It's the second time in the last week that she's pressed about my situation. The group all look at me, and I feel the pressure. Thankfully I also feel the warm sensation of the second large glass of chardonnay in my bloodstream, and I'm ready to reveal a little bit.

'Lil's dad isn't in the picture. It's only her and me at home.' I take another sip of my wine. 'My neighbour is lovely though, and she helps me out quite a bit.'

'Does he see Lila at all?' Marnie asks.

'He tries. But no.'

The other women look at me expectantly. But I'm not ready to share any more.

Then right on cue, my darling daughter saves me, letting out a loud cry from the pram. 'I should get this little one home,' I say, emptying my glass in one large swig. 'Same time next week?'

I'm shocked at myself for even asking. Shocked and proud. Maybe I should drink before mothers' group. *Is that the only way I can make friends?*

My question is met with a series of yes, definitely and can't wait. The sound of it making my heart beat a tiny bit faster. Was it finally happening? Is this what my mum was talking about?

Chapter 12

Fleur

Drinks had been a great idea until it was only Marnie and me left at the surf club. We settle the bill, and I walk with Marnie back to the community centre.

My anger has resurfaced now that it's just us. Too many glasses of wine aren't helping. My good hand grips the pram tightly, my knuckles turning white.

We stop near Marnie's car and I turn to her. 'What the hell was that in there earlier?'

'What?' Marnie says, hurt and shock in her eyes.

'Patting my knee in mothers' group. Giving the impression that Aaron isn't there for me.'

'I-I was trying to be supportive. I'm sorry.'

'Why would I need your support? My husband's not the one working night shift and going out late on the weekend.' I'm almost yelling now, and I lower my voice, conscious of the people passing by. 'You know nothing about Aaron.'

Marnie looks down at her hands. She fidgets with a strap on the pram. She's silent for so long, I don't know if the conversation is over or if she's thinking carefully about what to say next. Turns out it's the latter.

'Fleur, you know you can tell me anything, yeah? If things are hard, you can trust me.'

I'm just about reaching boiling point, and then it hits me. She knows.

'What did Rob say to you?'

Marnie looks taken aback. 'What? Nothing.'

'Don't lie to me, Marnie.'

She sighs. 'He mentioned he had to drop by your place on the weekend, and I've been worried about you.'

'He shouldn't be telling you anything about my private business,' I snap. 'Besides, there's nothing to be worried about.'

'But what about your hand? What really happened?'

I let out a frustrated groan. 'Like I told Rob, I wasn't paying attention while I was ironing.'

She purses her lips. She's not buying it.

'Anyway, thanks for your concern.' My tone is lined with sarcasm. 'I need to get Mia home.'

I storm off. My car is a little further away, and I resist the urge to turn back. I need to hide my burning cheeks.

How dare she try to meddle in my and Aaron's relationship. Rob has crossed a line. She's crossed a line. And to so publicly try to comfort me! I work my ass off to show the world that I'm fine. That I'm happily married to my high school sweetheart. That I'm totally nailing motherhood, and I don't have a worry in the world.

For all the pain Aaron puts me through, I have nothing without him. He loves our daughter, and he puts food on the table, even if it isn't much. What would I do without him?

I get home feeling defensive of Aaron and excited to see him. I barely recognise this pathetic version of myself. Skipping through the front door with Mia in my arms, I expect to see him sprawled out on the couch with a beer in his hand. He said he was knocking off early today.

I don't even care what he's doing. I need to see him. Instead, I find a note on the kitchen bench.

I'VE GONE OUT BECAUSE THIS HOUSE IS DISGUSTING. FIX IT.

I blink back tears. I'll have to do better.

Chapter 13

Peyton

Mum looks at me as though I've asked for a kidney.

'Peyton, you've been out late twice this week. You're a mother now. Start acting like one.'

'You're the one who told me I need to make some friends. And I have. One girl in my mothers' group goes to the club.'

'That's great. Why don't you organise a time to catch up *with* your babies?'

'I did actually,' I admit. I was happy with myself for suggesting drinks at the surf club. Besides the run in with an old school mate, the afternoon had been fun. I enjoyed listening to the other women bag out their useless husbands and have a laugh. Maybe I wasn't so badly off on my own. 'I organised drinks after our meeting today, and the babies joined us.' Not that they were aware of it. *Thank you for sleeping like a champ, Lucas!*

'Great, I'm glad,' Mum says, and I know she's being genuine. 'So why would you need to go for drinks again tonight?'

Ugh. She got me. But that's not the only reason I want to go out tonight.

The baby monitor screen flashes. Lucas is stirring. Thirty minutes exactly. Damn these catnaps. I huff as I leave Mum in the kitchen, acting as much a baby as my son. I spend fifteen minutes trying to resettle Lucas with no success. He's wide awake and sucking his hands, looking for milk.

'Come here, you little milk monster,' I say, lifting him out of his cot.

When I told Mum and Dad I was pregnant, they were shocked—Dad a little horrified. But it didn't take them long to come around and insist that I keep living at home. They cleared the master bedroom and swapped rooms with me. I didn't expect them to do that and made it clear that I didn't need their bedroom. But as I look around now, they were right. I needed the space. There's my bed, Lucas's cot, a nursing chair and, in the en suite bathroom, a portable change table. Everything I need is in this space, and it probably serves them well that I can keep to this room and not take over half of the house.

Sitting in the nursing chair Mum scored in Aldi's Special Buys, I feed Lucas. I'm so torn. I have this gorgeous son, supportive family and the perfect place to live, but I'm nineteen, and I want to go out. I want to meet people. I want to have fun and forget about my responsibilities. I don't want to be selfish and entitled, but I can't have a baby and suddenly age and mature ten years.

Tears fall down my cheeks on to Lucas' head as he nuzzles away, blissfully unaware.

'Knock, knock.' Mum pops her head in. 'Oh Peyt, honey, what's wrong?' She rushes over and sits on the bed opposite me.

My silent tears turn to shoulder heaving sobs. Lucas pulls away and cries, unimpressed with the interruption to his afternoon tea.

'Pass him here. I'll burp him while you take a minute.'

I give Lucas to Mum and grab one of the burp cloths from next to me to wipe my face.

'I'm sorry, Mum. I know you probably think I'm a brat, but I don't know how to be a good mum and a teenager.'

She looks at me and smiles. The same warming, motherly smile she has given me since I was a child. 'You're a great mum. The fact you're so worried about being a good mum is what makes you one.'

Lucas burps, and Mum hands him back to me. He latches easily and continues his feed.

'But there's no perfect time or way to have a baby,' she continues. 'Certainly being young and single is challenging, but you have so much support. I found it hard to switch off from work when your brother was born, and I felt selfish and like a terrible mum. It's hard to give up a part of yourself when you become a parent, and it's fine to not want to let that part of yourself go.'

It's strange hearing my mum say this because I've never known her as anything but Mum. I never thought about the fact that, once upon a time, she may have had different hopes and dreams.

'I love Lucas, but I feel like I'm missing out on so much,' I say.

She shrugs and looks at Lucas. 'Yeah but look at what you've gained as well.'

I look down. As if right on cue, his little hand tickles my shoulder. I let out some sort of laugh-sob combination. I'd never trade this.

'Anyway, I've spoken to your dad. We've agreed that we'll take Lucas one night a week. So you can go out tonight but then you're home all weekend, understand?'

It's more than I deserve. I nod and more tears come. 'Thanks, Mum.'

She kisses my forehead and leaves.

***

Dad drops me off at the club. I didn't ask Rob if he was hanging around after training. I wasn't going to be the one to start up the text back and forth again. Lucas was so unsettled tonight that I almost didn't come at all. My look ends up being a rushed make up job and unwashed hair up in a high pony. That, along with my denim shorts and plain white tee, means I'm super casual compared to Saturday night.

I grab a cider and head outside. The usual group of guys is sitting at one of the tables. My pulse races when I see Rob sitting with them. He doesn't see me. At another table sits Amalia and a few other people I've seen before but don't know well. She waves me over and introduces me. Mostly they're the wives or girlfriends of the guys at Rob's table.

I rarely hang out with the women at the club, and I feel pressure to make conversation with Amalia while the others chatter amongst themselves.

'Mothers' group was awkward today, hey?' I ask.

I immediately regret my question, remembering that Amalia didn't respond to Liz's question at all. She sips her drink.

I panic. 'You know, with Hanbi and Zara clashing, and Fleur acting weird?'

She relaxes her shoulders and half smiles. 'Yeah, super awkward. Zara sure knows how to get under people's skin.'

'Tell me about it.' I try to let the conversation flow naturally, but it isn't happening. I take a long sip of my drink.

'I was impressed by you though,' Amalia smiles. 'Young, single mum raising Lucas on your own.'

As she says it, I'm distracted by Rob, who walks past. He smiles at me and my insides heat. I hope he didn't overhear that. Single mum is probably a massive turn-off.

'I guess I'm not the only one impressed by you though. But for different reasons.' She laughs and my cheeks flush.

'I'm so embarrassed you saw that the other night.'

'Oh, don't be. You're entitled to a little fun.'

'Thanks. And thanks for what you said. Although, I'm definitely not on my own. My parents are lifesavers.'

Amalia nods. Sadness flashes across her eyes.

'You're okay, right?' I ask, remembering she only has her neighbour and didn't share much about Lila's dad.

She looks down at her glass for what feels like an eternity. When she looks up, she's bright eyed and smiling, a totally different person to a moment ago. 'Of course.' She lifts her glass. 'I need a refill.'

Amalia goes to the bar, and I head to the ladies. My phone buzzes. It's Rob. I look around the clubhouse wondering if he's watching me.

`Meet me in the carpark.`

My heart races. I quickly use the bathroom and check my hair and makeup. I take a mint from my bag and head outside.

When my brother played here, my dad was on the board for the club and was always pushing for a carpark upgrade. It's muddy in winter but that didn't matter because the club is rarely used then. In summer, though, it's a dusty mess. Every time a car drives in or out, the dust kicks up and carries onto the field. You can't leave this ground without dust-stained whites. But he also had a problem with the lighting. 'For a place that hosts so many functions, how can you have no lights in the car park? It's dangerous.' He sounded like a broken record. It's been years, and still the carpark is a dusty paddock, and as I walk through it, it's pitch black. He was right. It's not safe at all.

'Hey,' a voice whispers from my left, and I jump. 'It's me.' Rob's silhouette is visible leaning against a car.

'Shit, you scared me. What are you doing out here in the dark?'

He grabs my hand and pulls me close to him. 'Sorry. I didn't think the clubhouse was the best place for what I want to do next.'

Rob places one hand firmly on the small of my back and draws me closer. The other hand brushes my cheek. My legs turn to jelly. He leans in and kisses me. The hand on my back pulls me closer, and I lift to my toes and put my arms around his neck. I lose myself for a few seconds before I pull away, short of breath.

'What's wrong?' he asks, his eyes greedy.

'I just. Nothing. Well, not nothing. It's not a big deal but why haven't you texted me back?'

Argh, I sound so needy. It's been two kisses. We're not married.

He cups my cheek. 'I'm sorry. I'm shocking with the phone. New job, crazy shifts, everyone's been neglected.' He kisses me softly on the cheek and I wonder who everyone includes. 'I'll try to do better.' The kisses continue from my cheek down to my neck, and my body can't help but forgive him.

I sigh loudly, which only encourages him. His lips are back on mine, his hands exploring under my t-shirt and up my back. When they move around to my front, I panic. My bra is packed with breast pads and the last person to go near my boobs was my milk guzzling son. I press myself hard up against him, forcing his hands back behind me. His back is firm against the car and as I push my body forward, I feel everything through his thin training shorts. He moans as I pulse my hips against him.

I'm getting so caught up in the moment when my mum's voice enters my head, reminding me I'm a mother. Here I am, about thirty seconds away from shagging this guy in his car. I need to stop.

I take a step back, my hands stay on his chest.

'Don't stop now.' His voice is low and breathless.

I smile. 'One of us has to be the strong one.' I peck his lips and leave him leaning against his car.

I don't want to be the strong one, but last time I let myself get too carried away, I ended up in one of my mate's beds. Nine months later, Lucas arrived. And he hasn't spoken to me since he found out I was pregnant. He ghosted me. It was his final year of high school. He was about to escape Lakesfield and head to Sydney for uni and parties and the famous Kings Cross nightlife. But it pissed me off that he had that option, and I didn't. Sure, I could've had an abortion, but when the doctor found Lucas' heartbeat when I was about eight weeks pregnant, an indescribable feeling washed over me, and I knew I had to have my baby, even if I was alone.

On my way back inside, headlights highlight my creased shirt and dishevelled pony tail. Rob is a few metres away and I know we must look seriously dodgy. The window goes down as it passes. It's Amalia. *Phew.*

'Another good night then?'

I shake my head and smile. 'See you next week.'

Amalia drives off. I have one last drink before heading home as well.

Chapter 14

Marnie

I feel guilty about what happened with Fleur on Thursday. What happens between her and her husband is none of my business, and Rob shouldn't be telling me things like that. He could get himself in trouble.

I've known the woman a little over a week. I don't owe her anything. I could forget about it and see her each week until the group fizzles out and I don't see her again. But I can't help but worry. I don't believe her story about the iron and I don't believe things are as great as she claims. That's why I text her on Saturday morning to catch up for another walk.

'Why are you getting involved, Marns? Leave it,' Rob says as he packs some snacks in his cricket bag.

'I want to clear the air with her and make sure she knows I'm here for her.'

'You've got your own issues. You don't need to take on someone else's.'

He's right but it stings to hear him say it. We've been together for so long. He knows I'm a worrier and knows about all the help I've had to get over the years. My head's been more of a mess since I fell pregnant. I'm definitely not handling motherhood. Our relationship is clearly strained and not the same. But I need to feel like I'm doing something meaningful. If I can't fix my life, maybe I can fix someone else's.

'I'm not taking on anything. We're going for a walk.'

'Just be careful. You don't need the stress.' Rob zips up his cricket bag and pecks me on the cheek. 'And please don't go to her house.'

'I won't. Good luck!' I call to him as he heads out the door.

He'll be gone all day. Why couldn't he play footy or basketball? A sport that doesn't go all day, every weekend. Not to mention the training. He came home late and in a foul mood on Thursday night. He tried to get me to take a shower with him, suggesting ways I could make him feel better. When I said no, he took a long shower alone and has barely said a word to me until now.

I load Jasper into the pram and head out to meet Fleur. She's beaten me to our meeting spot again. I check my watch; I'm early. This girl always seems to have everything in control. Maybe she's not struggling after all. Or perhaps this is her way of hiding how bad it is.

She smiles when I approach. 'Morning,' she says in her usual chipper voice. Most of her face is hiding behind her dark sunglasses. Straight hair falls perfectly down her back and her long sleeve sports top and leggings hug her tiny figure. And she still has a bandage on her hand.

'Hey,' I pause, feeling awkward. We both go to speak but she stops. 'Look, I'm sorry about the other day. It's none of my business.'

'Don't worry about it,' she says, flicking a hand as though she's flicking away the issue. 'I can understand why you may have worried, but your husband was wasting his time at our place. Big misunderstanding, I guess.'

She says it so confidently, but I don't miss the way she lets go of the pram and bends and flexes the fingers on her bandaged hand.

'How's it feeling?' I nod toward her hand and she quickly grabs the handle of the pram again.

'Yeah, it's fine. Just a minor burn. Keeping it wrapped up, so it doesn't get infected.'

'Have you had it looked at?'

'Nah, no need. I was a nurse before I had Mia. I can treat it myself.'

My gut churns at that. It doesn't sit well that she has a mysterious injury that she's treating herself, even if she does have some level of expertise. But I use it as an out to change the subject.

'Nursing? Nice. Where did you work?'

'At the hospital in the next town. I worked in a big hospital in Melbourne to start. Definitely a much quieter job out here.'

'Yeah, I imagine so.' I remember our own life in Melbourne before coming out here for Rob's work—so different. 'Where in Melbourne did you live?'

'Near the city.' Fleur smiles, her gaze distant as she pushes the pram alongside me. 'Oh, we had so much fun back then going to all the amazing restaurants and bars.' She looks over at me. 'Bit different now with the baby in a small town, right?'

I nod. 'Sure is. We used to live in the outer northern suburbs but would head into town a lot for a drink or a show.' I miss Melbourne.

'What did you do back in the city?'

'I'm a teacher. We moved a week after Jasper was born, so I'd already finished up at my job.'

'Whoa! Moving house with a one-week-old, that's hectic.'

'That's cop life, I'm afraid.'

'What grade did you teach?'

'Grade six. Was so sad to miss the kids graduate at the end of last year.'

In early December, I had Jasper, so I finished up with my class at the end of term three. I'd hoped to pop back for their big graduation night but then Rob got promoted and before I knew it, we were packed and gone. Travelling back with a newborn was not going to happen. I wasn't up for attending local appointments, so Melbourne was certainly out of the question. I'd been upset that night. It was one of the first moments where I felt my old life disappear before my eyes.

'Do you miss it?' Fleur asks.

'What? Melbourne or my job?' I shrug. 'Both, a lot. I wanted to be a mum for so long, and I'm so grateful for Jasper. But not teaching this year feels like a big part of me is gone.'

Fleur stops walking. I pull up beside her.

'Everything okay?'

'Yeah,' she replies. 'That's true, isn't it? You lose a big part of your old self to become a mum.'

'Do you miss nursing?'

'Yeah. And I miss a lot of things from my life in Melbourne.'

Fleur walks again, and I wonder how different her life was back then. Did she end up with police officers on her doorstep and bandages on her body back then?

'Well, at least we found each other out here,' I say, and I half expect another one of Fleur's hugs. Am I actually making a friend? Surely I'm too old and boring for the stunning, upbeat Fleur. 'Couple of ex-Melbourne girls, pushing their babies around, dreaming of a city coffee or cocktail.'

Fleur laughs. 'Tell me if you find a coffee place even half as decent as a Melbourne cafe.'

'It doesn't exist.'

We continue around the park and even stop to let Jasper and Mia have a roll around on the grass. The conversation stays safe. We don't talk any more about the past or our partners or the jobs we mourn.

But when Fleur puts Mia back in the pram to leave, I can't help myself.

'Call me if you need anything, day or night, yeah? Keep safe.'

'Drop it, Marnie. I'm fine.' And she walks off.

Chapter 15

Amalia

I take Lila to the park on Saturday morning for some quiet time, just her and me. The week has been hectic. Thursday with the other mums was nice. But every other day this week has been busy. So busy that Lila has been my poor little shadow who's had to follow me around running errands. She's handled it like a boss though, sleeping in her pram or the car and happily playing on the go.

The thing is, I realised after Marcus' visit last Saturday that I need to find a way to get him out of my life for good. I hate him for what he did to me, to us. I'd be happy to never see his lying, cheating face again. The only reason I keep him around is because I need the financial support. On Monday I made an appointment in a nearby town that had a Centrelink office and organised to meet with someone to discuss what financial assistance I was eligible for. After sorting that out, I started job hunting for something casual about town. Mrs Casci has been more than happy to help with babysitting when I asked her. It wasn't going to be easy, but the sooner I could get rid of Marcus the better.

Finding a great little spot in the shade, I spread out a picnic rug near the lake. I love watching the ducks swim and dive in the water, hoping for someone to throw them the crust of their sandwich. It brings back memories of Mum. She used to take me to see the ducks all the times when I was little. We'd take stale bread with us and throw it into the water and watch the ducks race each other for a bite. Mum knew all kinds of interesting, weird facts about everything. She told me once that ducks have accents depending on if they're city ducks or country ducks. I found this hilarious. Mum and I proceeded to quack in various accents of our own, laughing until our cheeks hurt.

Tears prick at my eyes when I think about the memory. One day, I'll share these stories with Lila. I hope she finds duck accents equally funny. I lay her down on the picnic rug with a Sophie giraffe toy and an Oball. She grips the Oball proudly and holds it above her head, inspecting it carefully. I sit next to her and take a big gulp of the coffee I'd bought in town.

At the surf club on Thursday, Peyton created a WhatsApp group for our mothers' group. *Lakesfield Summer Mums*, she'd called it, and a flash of excitement shot through me when she'd added me. I like being a part of a group like that. I scroll through my phone. The first place I look is the WhatsApp group. It has become my new obsession. Better than Facebook or Instagram. The only thing is no one writes much. There'd been a little back and forth on Thursday when the group was first created.

Peyton: Welcome   Lakesfield   Summer Mums.

Fleur: Yay! Thanks for the add.

Marnie: Hi mamas.

Zara: I've never used WhatsApp before. I also rarely use my phone so forgive me if I'm quiet.

Amalia: Hi.

Peyton: Hanbi, I hope I added you correctly. I got your number from Liz.

Hanbi: Hey. Thanks. How were drinks?

Marnie: So nice. You really should try and get an extra hour off.

Hanbi: I wish! I'll see what I can do.

That was it for the evening. On Friday, there was more.

Fleur: I've had the worst night with Mia. How much coffee can I have while breastfeeding because basically, I need an IV hookup of the stuff.

Marnie: LOL! I feel ya.

Peyton: Mum says she drank coffee all the time when she had me. Soz, I know how annoying the whole 'When you were a baby...' comments can be.

Fleur: When they tell me what I want to hear, I'm all for it.

Zara: Hi mums. Be careful with caffeine consumption. I'm going to attach some articles about how it can affect your breastmilk and bub's development.

Three links followed. I didn't open them. No one thanked her.

Since then, there's been nothing else. But I keep checking, nevertheless.

As I'm scrolling, I notice two prams roll past on the path near the lake. Since becoming a mum, I'm drawn to prams. What brand? Does it convert to a double? How much storage space? Marcus and I hadn't bought our pram pre-scandal, so I had to fork out for that one on my own. That meant Lila had to make do with a second-hand cheap pram from Facebook marketplace. But I check out every pram that passes me, dreaming of upgrading one day.

Upon closer inspection, I realise that it's Marnie and Fleur walking around the park. My chest tightens and a lump forms in my throat. I'm hurt. Why are there mums catching up outside of mothers' group? There hadn't been an open invite in the WhatsApp group. Are all the mums forming closer bonds and catching up while I sit alone in the park with my baby? And if so, what's wrong with me? Maybe they think I'm rude or weird because I don't say a lot. But I'm trying. I really am.

Fleur and Marnie appear to be in deep conversation and don't even notice Lila and me. Sadness tugs at me as I wonder what they're talking about. I desperately wish I had someone to talk to. Sure, there's Kya, but she's at a different stage in life. She's good for getting me out of the house and out for a drink, but we don't talk, talk. Not properly. What I'd give to talk to one of the other mums about what happened to my mum and what happened with Marcus.

I don't have many, if any, friends anymore. Apparently cutting Marcus off from Lila is more outrageous than him cheating on me, and so all our friends took his side. They dropped me like a hot potato. *More like a hot mess.* Single mum, no job, no money, no friends.

Here's hoping one of these job applications is successful because that jerk needs to pay.

Chapter 16

Peyton

I'm dancing around my room, music blaring, sipping on a vodka Seltzer. It's a stunning summer day and Mum decided to take Lucas with her and Dad to see my nana in Melbourne. An entire twenty-four hours of freedom. Sure, I have to pump (thanks Mum for reminding me a hundred times) and yes I cried for the first hour after he left feeling guilty and missing him, but now I'm excited to be a nineteen-year-old with no responsibilities.

As I finish getting ready, I add the hum of the breast pump to the beat of my music. I sent Rob a text yesterday after our carpark hookup on Thursday, and we're going for dinner and drinks after his match today. I said I'd go down and catch the last few overs.

Choosing what to wear to an afternoon at the cricket club that's also suitable for Saturday night drinks is tough. I settle for a linen wraparound dress that shows the perfect amount of cleavage and legs and some white sneakers.

***

The cricket club is busy when I arrive. There's about an hour of play left and apparently the team is playing well. It's such a nice day that lots of people have come down to watch. I used to be so into it when my brother played, watching each ball and getting caught up in every run and every umpiring decision. Then that became less cool as I got older, and I was more interested in the social side of it. Now, the cheap drinks and checking Rob out in his whites are more than enough to get me here.

I grab myself a cider and look around for somewhere to watch from.

'Peyt!'

I turn to see Bree waving me over. She's standing in a group of the usual club regulars. I so can't be bothered talking to her but being in a big group at least means the conversation isn't all up to me.

'Hey,' I say as I approach Bree and the group.

'We only need two more wickets to win. The other team needs a fair few runs,' Bree says, as though she's part of the team. 'We've got this, I reckon.'

'Great.' I try to sound interested, but my eyes are scanning the field for Rob. He's fielding on the boundary way out on the other side of the field. Damn!

I spend the next half hour taking part in painful small talk with Bree and watching as Rob and the team bowl the remaining batsmen out. I half-heartedly join in the clapping and cheering as the team walks off, but mostly I'm staring at Rob. His tanned, toned arms flex as he claps off his teammates.

*＊＊

Rob drives us to a restaurant just out of town. There are plenty to choose from that we could walk to and then Rob could have a couple of drinks, but he insists.

'I like the steak here,' he says to explain himself.

I roll my eyes. Old guys and their steaks, right?

We sit at a table out the front of the small restaurant. There's a cool breeze that makes the warm night bearable. It's certainly nothing fancy, with cheap outdoor chairs and a table that rocks on its uneven legs. There's a sheet of paper across the top of the table acting as a tablecloth, which, judging from a table nearby that is occupied by a family, doubles as a giant sketchpad for kids with crayons.

'Can I get you some drinks?' the waitress asks us. She's about my age, and I can't help but envy her, probably working a summer job before uni starts. No responsibilities, living her life.

I flick through the cocktail menu. 'I'll have an Amaretto sour please.'

'Beer for me, thanks,' Rob says.

Rob and I look at the food menu. Dating is foreign to me. I went on occasional dates in high school but that involved getting a Boost Juice or seeing a movie. Not dinner. The silence is awkward. Besides a few hookups at the cricket club and some texts, we haven't really spoken to each other. I loathe small talk, but I hate awkward silences even more. I look up from my menu to say something and he starts to speak at the same time.

I smile. 'You go.'

'I was going to ask what you were thinking of ordering,' Rob says.

Ugh. There's the small talk.

'The seafood pasta sounds good, probably that. Are you getting your precious steak?'

He laughs. 'Hey, it's a Black Angus. It's good.'

I shake my head. I have no idea what that even means.

The waitress returns with our drinks. She places them on the table and immediately the condensation makes wet rings on the paper—classy. Then she takes our orders.

I sip my cocktail and watch as the cars pass, heading towards town. Probably heading to where most people go to eat and drink on a Saturday night.

'So what do you do for fun?' Rob asks, and I almost spit out my drink. Maybe I'm not the only one new to the dating thing.

As well as his question being so lame, I have no idea how to answer it. I don't work or study. I don't have much of a life at all besides looking after Lucas. It's embarrassing.

'Oh, I'm in between things at the moment. Not sure what I want to do yet.'

'You're young. You've got plenty of time to decide.'

'Yeah, I guess so.' I force a smile because it's such a parent thing to say. 'Did you always want to be a cop?'

'Yep. One of those childhood dreams. Played with toy police cars when I was little and cops and robbers in the school playground. Never thought to do anything else.'

'How long have you been one?'

'I worked in Melbourne for ten years before transferring here a little over a month ago.'

I nod while silently trying to calculate how old that'd make him.

'Sarge,' a voice calls from behind me on the street.

Rob's eyes widen. Two cops approach the table.

'Hartlett, Mason,' Rob nods to each of the officers. 'What are you doing out here?'

'Just patrolling,' the female officer responds. Her badge says Constable Mason. The other officer is a Senior Constable. I guess that makes Rob their boss.

The police officers look from Rob to me, and I wait for him to introduce me. The silence becomes deafening. 'I'm—'

Rob cuts me off. 'This is a friend from Melbourne.'

The woman tilts her head slightly.

'Lisa Mason.' The male officer points at his partner before pointing at himself. 'Jack Hartlett. We better get back to it,' he says. 'Nice to meet you.'

I open my mouth to respond and Rob cuts me off. 'See you at the station.'

Hartlett and Mason walk away.

'A friend from Melbourne?' I ask, a little annoyed at the lie.

'Sorry, I didn't want them getting your name. They're cops. They'll suss you out.'

I laugh. 'Suss me out?'

Rob's saved by the waitress who places our meals down in front of us.

***

'You live here?' Rob asks, looking at my parents' house as we pull up. 'It's huge.'

'Yeah, between things remember,' I respond, feeling embarrassed. 'I still live with my parents.' I watch his face to see his reaction, but he doesn't seem to care. 'Did you want to come in?'

His face flushes as he stumbles over an answer.

'They aren't home,' I quickly add.

He visibly relaxes. Then he looks at his phone and hesitates before agreeing to come inside.

I stop him at the front door. *Shit, shit, shit.* The house is going to be a dead giveaway that I have a baby. Maybe I can say my parents had a late, happy accident. My mind is racing.

'Wait here a sec,' I say and close the front door with Rob left standing on the porch.

I can keep him to one end of the house and clear it of anything baby-like. I run around madly picking up bottles, blankets and toys so that the lounge, kitchen and bathroom are free of anything to do with Lucas. A pang of guilt ripples through me for trying to deny his existence. But then Rob knocks on the door and I rush to answer. I'll be a good mum tomorrow.

We get comfortable on the couch with a bottle of Mum's wine. I reach for the remote and flick through movie options.

'Netflix and chill?' Rob says.

I choke on my wine, laughing. 'That's very presumptuous of you.'

His forehead creases, and colour flushes into his cheeks. 'I'm guessing there's a hidden meaning I don't know about.'

I'm still laughing as I nod. 'You never know though.' I run my tongue over my lip.

Rob inches closer. He smells incredible. My insides flutter, and then there's a familiar prickling feeling in my full breasts. I panic and jump up.

'Pick something to watch. I'll be back in ten. Forgot to do something for Mum.'

I rush out, leaving him with a blank stare on his face.

When I return, he's watching *Die Hard*, the most middle-aged dude film ever. I've pumped and now pray that's enough to not squirt anyone who comes near. Talk about a mood killer. And one with a fair bit of explaining to do.

I snuggle in close to Rob, pretending to be keen on the movie. I place my hand on his thigh and slowly stroke it. His breath hitches, and he sighs. I move my hand higher over his thin shorts, inching closer to what I really want.

Clearly unwilling to wait, Rob turns to me and pulls me on top of him. My legs are on either side of him, and I shudder as he strokes his hands down my back. I look down at him and hunger burns in his eyes. Then our lips meet, and he doesn't hold back.

Chapter 17

Marnie

The smell of bacon and coffee wakes me up before the sound of Jasper's cries. I look at his bassinet next to me and he's gone. I bolt upright before Rob enters the room with a tray and a goofy smile on his face.

'Where's Jasper?'

'I thought I'd give you a sleep in. I've been working so much, and you need a break.'

I rub my eyes. Eight thirty flashes on my phone screen. I gasp.

'That's a huge sleep in. What did you feed him?' What the hell is going on? His moods are so up and down. I barely know how to respond.

'Found some expressed milk in the freezer. He's back asleep in his own room now.'

I hardly believe what I'm hearing. My son, the fusspot, has gone down in his own room. Surely not.

'Anyway, I've made you breakfast. Bacon, eggs and coffee.'

'Wow. I could get used to this.' I smile. 'Thank you.' I sip my coffee. 'Where were you last night?'

Rob came in at two o'clock last night. I pretended to be asleep because I didn't want to speak and wake Jasper, who slept quietly beside me.

He runs a hand through his hair. 'I stayed back at the club for a few drinks. Didn't you get my text?'

He had sent me a message, but the club closes at midnight. That's when their liquor licence ends. I only know that because Rob himself looked into it. He has to be careful now that he's the local sergeant.

'Yeah, I did. But you were home well after twelve.'

'I didn't know I had a curfew,' Rob snaps, suddenly defensive. 'I went to a mate's house afterwards.'

I guess the pleasant morning was nice while it lasted. This must be a *'free me of guilt'* sleep in and breakfast. And to be fair, a sleep in and breakfast could forgive a lot of things these days.

Jasper cries out and that halts our conversation before it becomes too heated.

'I'll get him,' Rob says. 'You eat.'

***

After breakfast, we head out for a walk in the parklands. We stop at the cafe to pick up some more coffee first. As we walk in, two police officers come out. I manoeuvre the pram out of their way but not without bashing it against the door frame and knocking poor Jasper around.

'Sarge. Out and about again, mate?' the male officer says with a chuckle. His badge says Jack Hartlett.

Rob forces a laugh. 'Jack, Lisa, good to see you again.' He goes to walk into the cafe and I stand there a little dumbfounded. Why won't he introduce me to his colleagues?

'Again?' I ask, trying to force myself into the conversation, and Rob stops walking.

It's as if the officers only just notice that I'm there. The other officer, Lisa, I'm guessing, looks me up and down before turning to Rob. 'We ran into...'

Rob cuts her off. 'I saw them last night when they were on duty.'

I nod. It makes sense. They were probably patrolling and swung by the club. I clear my throat, staring at Rob.

'Um, this is my wife Marnie,' he says. 'Marnie, this is Constable Lisa Mason and Senior Constable Jack Hartlett, colleagues of mine.'

Lisa's eyes narrow at me before she turns to Rob to speak. She's cut off again, this time by her partner.

'Lovely to meet you, Mrs Jones. And this must be Jasper.' Jack says, looking into the pram. 'We've heard a lot about him.'

Lisa says nothing, staring at Rob. It makes me uncomfortable.

'Anyway, we're grabbing coffee,' I say. 'Great to meet you.' I push the pram past Rob and into the cafe. He stays outside, talking to them.

While I wait for our coffees and Rob, the group WhatsApp message buzzes.

Peyton: *Hey. This may be TMI but is it normal to bleed when you have sex for the first time after having a baby?*

TMI? What the hell does that mean? I google the acronym, like I often do when scrolling various social media sites. Why can't people write the words? Too much information. Right. Well yeah, it's not something I'd share with the group. Not that I'd know, since I won't let Rob come near me.

Zara: *Totally fine. As long as it doesn't continue to bleed a heap, all good.*

Hanbi: I think we're missing the real point here—you go girl!

Peyton: LOL thanks. So weird but oh so good.

I smile at the message. Oh well. Good on her.

Chapter 18

Fleur

I unravel the bandage from my hand. It's been a little over a week since Aaron struck me with the iron. I've been redressing it daily, but it's still weeping from the blisters that cover almost my entire palm. I know I should get it checked now. But the thought of explaining this to a doctor or nurse terrifies me. I've been on the other end of these conversations. I know what they'll say behind my back. I know what they'll write in my file. Plus, if Aaron found out, it'd be ten times worse.

I'll give it until Sunday. That's two weeks. I smother the burn in antiseptic and wince at the stinging sensation. Then I bandage it back up.

I'm dreading mothers' group today. I've been cold with Marnie since our walk on Saturday. She's trying to be nice, but I wish she'd butt out. Besides, she isn't exactly living her best life. I see how she mourns her old life. Everyone has their demons, their secrets. Mine are just a little more dangerous, I guess.

I arrive at the community centre early. I want to get in and start feeding Mia without running into anyone in the carpark. People are less likely to pry in front of the entire group.

My plan works. I take a seat opposite Liz. Strategic. I won't be the first to share.

'That's always the first spot to be taken,' she laughs.

I smile and begin feeding Mia. The other mums come in and the chatter level in the room picks up. It seems everyone's becoming more comfortable with one another.

'Welcome back ladies. Today's focus is extremely important—mental health.'

I get a sick feeling in my stomach. What's she going to make us share with the group? Some of the other mums look nervous too, fidgeting and avoiding eye contact.

'Today we're going to share what has been our biggest challenge as a mum so far. It may be feeding, sleeping, giving up work, strains on relationships.'

My cheeks heat, and I take a sip from the water bottle I'd brought with me.

'It's important,' Liz continues, 'that you realise you're not alone in your struggles. Social media does you lovely ladies no favours. If Instagram is a newsfeed of how perfect everyone's life is, imagine this session as a newsfeed of what isn't perfect.'

I inwardly groan. A session of complaining, great.

'Fleur, since you were first to arrive, why don't you start us off?'

What! Dammit. She got me. There's no safe place to sit in here.

I flick my perfectly curled hair behind my shoulder and try to muster up some confidence. 'Hmm, the biggest challenge...' I let out a little laugh, 'It's gotta be the poo and the spew, right? It's non-stop.'

Some of the other mums laugh and nod. Liz doesn't look too impressed with my answer. 'Anything else that challenges you?'

Being broke. Being abused by my alcoholic husband. 'Nope. Oh, obviously sleep deprivation. I can't think straight half the time.'

Liz smiles. 'Definitely a common challenge.' She waits for more, but I look away to signal that I'm done. She takes the hint. 'What about you, Zara?'

I expect Zara to say she has no challenges. That her exclusively breastfed baby is perfect in every way, and she can't wait to get home to kiss her supportive soulmate husband.

But she says nothing. She shakes her head. Maybe not everything is perfect in paradise.

'Of course, there's no obligation to share. Hanbi?'

Hanbi is dressed in casual clothes today, not her usual professional look. She looks exhausted.

'Biggest challenge is definitely going back to work. My partner is great and does the night feeds with bottles and looks after Sienna during the day but I'm still tired. And I know people are judging me, trying to make me feel guilty about going back so soon.'

I feel for Hanbi. Why can't the woman be the sole breadwinner in a family? Why is it a woman's responsibility to stay at home with the baby? I admire her for breaking the stereotype. And I think she deserves to know.

'I think it's great you've gone back to work,' I say. 'What a strong female role model you are for Sienna.' And what a terribly pathetic one I am for Mia.

Hanbi smiles, her eyes full of gratitude. 'Thanks, Fleur. Anyway, my husband is sick, so I'm not working today. Mummy-daughter day, wish me luck!'

Liz looks to Peyton, who's next in the circle.

Peyton always looks stunning with her long red hair and perfect skin. Oh, to be that young again when you don't have to worry about makeup and the weight just falls off you. And apparently, I'm not the only one who thinks she looks great based on her WhatsApp messages over the weekend. I couldn't think of anything worse than having sex right now. It still hurts down there, and I'm exhausted. Of course, that doesn't stop Aaron if he's in the mood. It doesn't matter what I want.

'Being young is the biggest challenge for me. I don't have any friends my age going through this. They're all partying and travelling, and it sucks sometimes.'

'Plenty of time to party and travel when Lucas is older,' Liz winks at Peyton, 'and grown up kids make great designated drivers.'

Peyton smiles and looks down at a sleeping Lucas in her arms. 'Sounds good to me, buddy.'

'Marnie?' Liz asks.

I wonder if Marnie will tell the group how she's truly going. Will she share how she feels about losing a big part of her identity when she had Jasper? Will she admit she misses work? Will she tell the group that her marriage is strained?

'Oh, sleep deprivation, as Fleur said.' She looks at me, and I know straight away she isn't going to share anything deep and meaningful. 'And having a partner who works night shifts. It can make the juggle a little tricky, but we're getting there.'

The last person in the group to share is Amalia. She hasn't said a word in any of our sessions yet.

'Ummm, loneliness. I feel isolated as a mum now. It's not as easy to maintain friendships with people who don't have kids.'

I nod. I made some friends at the new hospital when I moved, but they're younger and single and don't care much about hanging out at my place while I breastfeed and change nappies in front of them.

Amalia continues. 'And illness has been a real challenge for us. Lila always seems to have a sniffly nose.'

'Do you have a diffuser?' Marnie asks.

'Yeah, but I never have it on.'

'I've got some fantastic essential oils for congestion. Perfectly fine for babies.'

'I'll have to get the name of the stuff.'

'Nope,' Marnie says, 'you can have some of mine. I used to have some pumping through my classroom during flu season. Still got heaps of it left.'

'Thanks.' Amalia's shoulders relax. I wonder if she is relieved to have finally shared or relieved to get some help for Lila. Probably both.

'Mothers' group can be a great solution to a few of your problems,' Liz says. 'You're in the thick of it together and knowing you're not alone can help a lot. If you're lonely—whether you're married or not, it happens—call on each other. Peyton asked me for a number the other day. Can I assume you're all in contact?'

'Yep,' Peyton says. 'We have a group message going.' Her cheeks turn pink and a smile pulls at the corner of her lips. I know what she's thinking about—her most recent message.

'Excellent,' Liz says.

Liz spends the next half hour describing the signs of post-natal depression and anxiety and explaining what services are available for us. Apparently, more than one in every seven new mums will suffer from post-natal depression. So statistically, one of us in this room is struggling right now. When Liz rattled off different signs and symptoms, I could honestly recognise some of them in most of the women in this room, including myself. I wonder if anyone else puts more effort into how they look at mothers' group to give the perception of coping? Does anyone else exhaust all their energy being positive in public? Liz hands around more flyers. I usually stuff them into the nappy bag, never to be seen again. But today, I carefully fold them and place them in the front pocket of the bag.

When I get home, I store the flyers where Aaron won't find them. I don't want him to think I'm not coping or that I'm talking to anyone about our relationship. That'd only make things worse. All Aaron needs is to be reminded that his family loves him. At least this is what

I try to tell myself. He works hard and stresses and does these stupid things because he wants what's best for us.

I take some frozen chicken breasts out of the freezer. Chicken Parma is one of Aaron's favourite meals. I'll cook that tonight and he'll know how much I care. He'll know that I'm not angry with him.

Chapter 19

Marnie

Mothers' group was a joke today. Well, mostly anyway. I know I was definitely lying. And Fleur was lying. Pretending we're doing better than we actually are. I saw Fleur take care to put the flyers in her bag this week. Maybe she'll ask for help. I've put mine away for safekeeping too, even though I'm currently receiving help. The midwives considered me at risk of post-natal depression early and referred me to a whole heap of professionals. I've only started medication recently, and I'm hopeful things will pick up soon. Especially with Rob. He's more distant than ever.

Before we leave the room, I catch Amalia.

'If you're free now, did you want to come and get that essential oil? You and Lila can pop in for a coffee?' As I say it, I rack my brain to remember if we even have coffee in the house, or milk. I'm sure there'll be something.

'Are you sure? Are we going for drinks today?'

I'd totally forgotten. Then I clear my throat and raise my voice so all the mums can hear. 'Ladies, drinks at mine today. I'll put my address in the group message.' A last-minute event at my place would usually send my anxiety sky high, but I'm finding company, and apparently wine, quite comforting lately.

Half an hour later, after a quick stop by the drive thru bottle shop and a frantic tidy up, the other mums are on my doorstep. Fleur said she couldn't make it because of some things to do around the house, but I'm sure she's avoiding me. Zara also posted in the group chat saying Tiana had fallen asleep in the car and she was planning to drive around for a while.

'Come in. Sorry, there are still a few boxes around. Wine?' I ask.

A chorus of yes's follows plus a hell yes from Hanbi who's able to join us because she has the day off.

It's another gorgeous summer day, so I lead the mums straight outside to the backyard. I spread out a playmat on the lawn for the babies, and the other mums and I sit at the table on the patio.

'So Peyton,' Hanbi says, 'who's the lucky guy?' She waggles her eyebrows.

Peyton giggles. 'Oh no one. The bleeding has stopped, no more details necessary.'

'Oh, come on. Let me live vicariously through you. I miss my youth,' she says with a laugh.

I agree with Hanbi. I can't imagine going out and hooking up with guys but I want to hear all about it. However, the subject changes and we're back on the topic of husband complaining.

We finish our first wine as Hanbi's phone buzzes. 'Son of a bitch. He's hopeless.'

'Everything okay?' I ask.

'Man flu. My husband is painful when he's sick. I'm going to have to head off and play nurse.'

'I'm sorry, Marnie,' Peyton says. 'But I think I need to go too.' She gestures at Lucas who is laying on the playmat, his nose dribbling away. 'Lucas hasn't stopped sneezing since we got here.'

'That's okay. Hope Lucas is alright. See you next week.'

That leaves Amalia. I top up our wines and sit back at the table with her.

She spins an oversized leather watch around her wrist.

'Nice watch,' I say, even though it's miles too big and masculine for her.

'Thanks. It was my dad's.'

A stab of guilt hits me in the chest for having judged her taste.

'He died in a car accident when I was a few weeks old. My mum gave it to me when I turned thirteen and I've worn it every day since.'

This is the most I've heard her speak, and I'm afraid I might burst into tears the first time she opens up. She undoes the clasp on the watch. Then she turns it over in her hand so that I can see the back of the face. It's engraved. *For my darling, A.*

'Dad's name was Andrew. Mum gave him this on their wedding day.'

'I'm so sorry you never got to know your dad. That must've been so hard on your mum.'

'Going through this parenting thing on my own now makes me appreciate how tough things must've been for her.'

'You're both strong women, that's for sure.' I didn't realise how alone she was. She'd said last week that Lila's dad was out of the picture and her neighbour was helpful, but that's not a heap of support.

Amalia smiles then. 'But then when I started kindergarten, Mum met another single mum, Michelle, whose daughter was in my class. They bonded instantly over their similar situations.'

'That would've been so nice to have that support.'

She nods. 'The other girl, Lily, was my best friend.' Amalia's voice sounds younger, happier. 'I actually named Lila after her. Lily and her mum were at our place every day, or we were at theirs. We went on trips together. We were basically like sisters.'

'Do you still see Lily?'

Amalia's face drops. She takes a deep breath. 'Not long after I turned fifteen, Lily and Michelle moved to America. My mum didn't handle it well. I think it was like losing her soulmate and a child.' She spins the watch around her wrist. 'She spiralled quickly. Drugs, alcohol. A neighbour found her in bed surrounded by pill bottles and a note a few weeks before my sixteenth birthday.'

My stomach churns, and I blink back the tears. 'Oh my, Amalia. I'm so sorry.' I place a hand over hers on the table.

'Thanks. It's been tough to have Lila without her here.'

'I can't even imagine. I'm constantly calling my mum for advice.' Once I even put the phone to Jasper's mouth so she could tell me whether she thought his breathing sounded okay. But I don't tell Amalia that. She doesn't need to know how neurotic I am.

She shrugs. I feel an overwhelming maternal instinct to look after Amalia. She's probably only a few years younger than me, but it's not fair that she doesn't have people to help her.

Jasper grizzles from the playmat, and we both agree that it's beginning to get too warm for the babies in the sun. We take our wines inside and sit in the living room. Jasper's only two months old and already our living room has been taken over by toys. The coffee table is pushed to one side and a big foam mat has taken its place in the centre of the room. There's a bouncer and an activity gym with different toys hanging down that make sounds or flash, and books everywhere. *If you read one book per day to your child, they'll have been read 1,825 books by the time they start school.* That's the primary school teacher in me, obsessed with books.

He isn't moving around yet, but I've prepared for that already, pushing back the objects he can reach for and pull off the shelves. Photos of Rob and I from our wedding and various holidays now sit pushed up against the wall rather than centred nicely on the shelf. I've put soft covers on the corners of the table and secured the bookcase to the wall. I'll never forget the episode of *Grey's Anatomy* when Dr Bailey's son gets crushed by a bookcase. Television tends to trigger a lot of my anxiety.

Lila lays under the play gym, kicking up at a ball that's hanging down and it jingles with each kick. She giggles every time it makes a noise. Amalia is staring at the shelves of photos.

'Oh, don't judge me for getting ahead with my baby proofing.' My cheeks flush. 'I'm so paranoid about him grabbing things one day.'

Amalia smiles. 'No, I'm not judging. That's a good idea. I'm admiring your photos. Is that your husband?'

'Yeah, that's Rob. We were such babies on our wedding day. But there are a few more recent travel snaps over here.'

I point to another shelf behind her where the photos continue. Amalia turns to look and her brow furrows.

'Everything okay?' I ask.

She hesitates. 'Um, yeah. Sorry.' There's a pause. 'It's bringing back memories of some of my own travel adventures.' She looks at her watch and gets up. 'I should be going. Thanks for the wine.'

'Wait, let me get that oil for you.'

I grab the essential oil from Jasper's room and give it to Amalia. 'One drop in some water should be plenty—it's strong.'

'Thanks so much.' She glances back at the photos one last time. 'Take care, yeah?' She adds, her tone laced with concern.

I nod and close the door behind her. I go back to the family room. Her glass of wine sits on the coffee table, barely touched.

Chapter 20

Peyton

'Ew!!' I screw my face up as I use the aspirator to clear Lucas' nose.

'Don't be ridiculous, Peyt,' Mum says. 'He's your son. You're going to come across grosser things than a bit of baby snot.'

'But why do we have to suck it out? It's disgusting.'

'You think you can put a tissue to a tiny baby's nose and get him to blow? The poor thing needs some help.'

He woke up fine, and we went to mothers' group this morning. But since being at Marnie's, Lucas has been sniffling and unsettled when lying down. He only seems to be happy when he's feeding or sitting upright in my arms. Poor baby. I'm not sure if he's caught something or if it's an allergic reaction from lying on Marnie's lawn.

'You might be in for a long night I'm afraid. I remember when you and your brother were unwell and all you wanted was cuddles.'

I sigh loudly, feeling sorry for myself. I'm all for cuddles, and I want Lucas to feel better, but I haven't seen Rob since we did it on this very couch last weekend. And in the week that's past, I've barely heard from him. I'm not looking for a baby daddy, but some flirty texts make each day a little more exciting, and I can't stop thinking about him. I can definitely vouch for the fact that older guys have valuable experience. I shake my head, blocking the heated images racing through my mind. The same images I shut down earlier when Hanbi asked. Those women do not need a detailed play by play of my encounter with Rob.

Maybe I can go out for just an hour or two. Lucas loves cuddles from his Grandma too.

I put on my sweetest voice, 'Muuummm?'

'Nope. Not happening.'

'What! I didn't even say anything.'

'I know what you're going to ask me.'

I scowl. She knows me too well.

'Peyton, you need to stay home for Lucas tonight. Breastfeeding will do him good while he's congested.'

I roll my eyes. 'Fine. Here.' I pass Lucas to her. 'I should let Bree know I'm not coming.'

As if I'd be talking to Bree. I text Rob.

Hey babe. Can't make it to the club tonight. Was looking forward to another sneaky car park sesh.

I debate whether to add a winky face emoji. He's old. That generation love emojis. But I leave it at that. I take Lucas to the couch and start feeding him while Mum cooks dinner.

Lucas spends a long time feeding and fussing. His poor little blocked nose makes it so hard for him. I fear I could be glued to this couch for hours tonight.

The doorbell rings, and Mum's voice sings out from the kitchen. 'I'll get it.' Then a few moments later. 'Bree! How lovely to see you.'

Shit!

I quickly rush to the front door. Lucas is startled by the interruption and thrashes about in my arms as a big milk stain seeps through my singlet.

'Peyton said you two have been hanging out at the club together again. How are your parents?'

'Bree! Hi!' I interrupt.

'Hey. Thought we could walk up to the club together tonight.'

Mum looks at me, confused.

I begin to panic. 'Umm, didn't you get my text?'

Bree looks at her phone. 'Nope. What's up?'

'I can't make it tonight. Lucas is sick. Um, I guess my phone's playing up.'

'Oh, poor bubba.' She steps forward to gush at him before properly absorbing my words and quickly jumping back as though he has the plague. 'Hope he feels better. Hopefully you can come for a drink after the match on Saturday.'

'Sounds good.'

'See ya, Peyt. See ya Mrs B.'

Bree leaves, and I scurry back to the couch as though I haven't been caught in a lie.

'That's strange,' Mum says, entering the lounge. 'I saw you text her. You should check your phone.'

I pretend to click through my messages. 'Oh, oops. Looks like I forgot to hit send earlier.' I'm a terrible liar.

Mum's eyes narrow. 'Not like you to make a mistake when it comes to texting.'

A dig at me. But I laugh because I want this conversation over. The last thing I need is to be quizzed about who else I could be texting.

Mum goes back into the kitchen, and my phone buzzes. My heart races, hoping it's Rob.

Sorry, been busy with work this week but I haven't stopped thinking about Saturday night.

His text ends with a fire emoji. I smile. Standard Gen Y. We flirt back and forth for a few hours. Lucas is basically attached to me the entire time. Rob sends me a selfie from the cricket club. *Wish you were here.* He's barely said a word to me all week but now he's at the club, he's so chatty. Eventually I text him goodnight with a cute but G-rated photo of me in bed.

Chapter 21

Amalia

Snake. The new guy here is a lying snake. I want to shout it out from the rooftop of the clubhouse that he's a cheating bastard, but I'm a nobody. They wouldn't listen. It's a boys' club after all, and teammates are like brothers. You mess with one, you mess with all of them.

So, I watch from my table as Rob laughs with the guys, sips from his beer and smiles to himself as he taps away on his phone. I'm sitting with the usual group of girls. They all have husbands or boyfriends on the team, and I wonder what they'd say if I told them about Rob. Before I had Lila, I was working at one of the local bank branches. That's where I met Kya. She'd always drag me down here for a drink. Sometimes Lila's dad, Marcus, would come too. Throughout my pregnancy, I kept away, not wanting to discuss what happened. But now I'm back. Kya's the only friend Marcus didn't steal.

'Am, do you want another drink?' Kya asks as she gets up from her place at the table. She's a newlywed, still very much in the honeymoon phase. Everything is fun. Everything is exciting. Everything is an opportunity to dress up, go out and show off her handsome hubby, Mitch. There's a darkness deep inside me that often creeps up when I'm with Kya. I push it back down, trying to be grateful for her friendship. It's not just that I'm a little envious, I'm annoyed that she doesn't fit the role that I needed her to fill when Marcus and I broke up. I needed her to need me and only me. But her world revolves around Mitch. I'm jealous. My life is a mess. Perhaps not as messy as Rob's, but messy all the same.

I look down at my empty wine glass. 'Yes, please. Chardonnay, thanks.' I figure I can have one more before I need to feed Lil again.

Kya bounces over to Mitch, presumably to ask him the same thing, consolidating herself as the perfect wife in front of the boys. Her high-pitched laugh echoes across the balcony outside the clubhouse. Rob continues to stare at his phone. It's weird to think of the faces we must make when we read our phone. We assume nobody would stare at us, watching our every expression and reaction as we mindlessly scroll or text. But I'm staring, and his expression flicks from a playful smirk, where his lips purse and eyebrows lift slightly, to worry, when a crease between his eyebrows appears and he looks around sheepishly. Each time he looks around, I glance down at my own phone. It's almost predictable, the back and forth of his expression, and I'm certain that he's texting Peyton. I'm tempted to text her myself to confirm it. I'm glad she's not here though because I'm not ready to break the news to her. I'm not even sure I'll tell her at all.

Kya returns with my drink. 'Girl, it's so obvious that you're checking out the new guy.'

My cheeks burn. 'What? No, I'm not.' I sound far too defensive, probably because I was checking him out but not in the way she thinks.

'You're going red! Come on, let's go talk to him.' She goes to grab my hand, but I shake it off.

'No, I'm not interested. I know his wife.'

'He's hot,' Kya says, glancing over at him. 'I didn't realise he was married.'

'Yeah.' I sip my wine and desperately try to think of a way to change the subject.

Thankfully, Kya's attention span is as short as her dress tonight, and she unknowingly saves me. 'How's Lila going?'

'She's good. I'm hoping she'll sleep better tonight. One of the mums in my mothers' group gave me some essential oils to help her stuffy nose.'

I know Kya couldn't care less about babies and essential oils, but she nods away, feigning interest. 'Are the other mums cool?'

I choke back a laugh at the word 'cool'. How would I describe the other mums? Tired, exhausted, lost, neck deep in spew, poo and Sudocrem.

'Yeah, they seem nice.' I can't help but look back over at Rob. Too nice to have jerks like him upend their lives.

I rushed out on Marnie earlier and feel terrible about it. She's so lovely, and we got on well. It was easy to tell her about my dysfunctional family growing up. Michelle and my mum were not romantically involved, but I felt like I had two mums when I was younger and was the luckiest kid in the world. I didn't tell Marnie about what Mum's letter had said though.

My darling A. Like she'd called my dad. *You were my greatest gift. Find yourself a man like your dad and a friend like Michelle and don't let go.*

I'd been so mad at her for leaving me. For the longest time, I couldn't understand how she could do it, and I suppose I still don't. I tried to track down Michelle and Lily in the States, but it's like they didn't want to be found. They hadn't even called after Mum died.

The police officers who collected me from school the day that Mum died treated me like dirt. It was as though they viewed me only as an addict's daughter and not the innocent, terrified orphan that I'd suddenly become. They even questioned me to see if I knew Mum's supplier. From that day on, I didn't trust the police, or any adults really. I was placed in foster care, but nobody was keen on someone my age and with my background, so I spent my last two years of school in community housing. I was lucky that my mum, despite her demons, had saved a bit of money from Dad's life insurance. By the time I finished school, I was able to rent my own place. And through it all, I never forgot my mum's words. I was determined to find a man like my dad or a friend like Michelle.

Five years ago, I met Kya, but it didn't take me long to realise she wasn't my Michelle.

'Not as cool as me though,' Kya laughs, bringing me back to the present. She mockingly flicks her hair.

Not as cool, I think to myself. But you're no Michelle either.

***

When I get home, Mrs Casci heats up a bowl of pasta that she's made me.

'The rest is in the freezer, pet. You need to eat more.'

She is always commenting on how tiny I apparently am, and I am more than happy to enjoy her homemade pastas and lasagnes. She is an amazing cook.

'Thanks Nonna,' I say, and she smiles.

'I used the oil you showed me and Lila is sound asleep. Hopefully it helps.'

'I hope so too.'

'Do you need anything before I go?'

'No, you've done more than enough. Thank you.'

'My pleasure.'

Mrs Casci leaves. I eat the delicious pasta and scroll through my phone. My heart races when I see there are new messages in the WhatsApp group.

Peyton: *Hi mums. Just letting you know Lucas is a bit sick. I hope he didn't spread the love in Marnie's backyard today.*

Hanbi: *Oh no, poor bubba. Hopefully he handles it better than my husband who's apparently dying a slow painful death.*

Marnie: *Jasper is fine. Hope he's okay.*

Zara: *Sorry we didn't make it this arvo. Just remember to breastfeed as much as possible tonight. Keep his fluids up and your milk will do wonders for him.*

I wonder if the other mums are rolling their eyes as I am currently doing. Zara always has something to say.

Hanbi: *Maybe I should offer hubby a bottle of expressed milk if it's so wondrous. Haha!*

I laugh to myself. She's taking the piss and I love it.

Peyton: *Ewwwwwww. Have you guys tried your milk? I can't do it. It's too weird.*

Fleur: *Feel better Lucas!! And no, I haven't.*

Hanbi: *Nope.*

Zara: *Of course. So has Joe. There's nothing gross about it. It's beautiful.*

I quickly type my own reply.

Hi. Sorry to hear about Lucas. Lila is fine, and I'm happy to say she's the only one who has tried my breastmilk.

I put my bowl in the dishwasher, and there's a knock at the door. My chest tightens. Not again, surely. I open the door, and sure enough, it's Marcus. This time he barges straight in and past me to the living room we once shared. He sits on the couch where we used to sit together and binge watch TV series.

'Um, what do you want?' I snap. 'You need to leave.'

'No. This needs to stop. Amalia, we have a child. Lila needs both of her parents around.'

'I didn't have both of my parents around,' I snap. 'I'd rather Lila have one parent than two parents pretending to like each other.'

'I love you.'

I shake my head. 'If you loved me, you wouldn't have cheated on me.'

He groans. 'How many times do I have to apologise? It was a mistake.'

'Maybe one time is a mistake. What *you* did? That's an affair.'

He says nothing for a while. Then he speaks. 'One of the guys from work said he saw you handing your resume in at a few places on the strip during the week.'

'Yeah, so?'

'And Lucy, you remember her?'

Of course I remember her. She was *my* friend after all. My friend until he supposedly won the friends in the 'divorce settlement'. I nod.

'She said she saw you at the Centrelink office.'

'Do you have people spying on me?'

He rolls his eyes.

'Yes, I was applying for jobs, and yes, I was at Centrelink.'

'Do you need more money? I told you I'd pay more if you need it. Anything for Lila.'

I believe him. Marcus has a good job, and he earns a lot of money. I know he'd give me anything I asked for. But the one thing I want is for him to disappear off the face of the earth. I can't make that happen until I get a job and I haven't heard from any of the places I'd applied to yet.

'No, I don't need your money.'

'Well, I think you should focus on staying home with Lila.'

'I don't care what you think I should be doing.' My confidence surprises myself.

Unfortunately, it surprises Marcus too, and he isn't happy. He stands up, towering over me.

'She's my daughter too.' He slams his fist down on the back of the couch. I flinch. 'I won't let you do this.'

'You need to leave.'

'I didn't want it to be like this.' He looks at me, his eyes downcast. 'You'll be hearing from my lawyer.'

Chapter 22

Fleur

Once again, I inspect the damage to my hand. I don't think it'll scar. The skin is red and tender, but the blisters look better. I'm tempted to wrap it back up, but I know it needs some fresh air now the risk of infection is gone.

Aaron and I haven't discussed the iron incident. I've been walking around the house with a bandaged hand for two weeks now and he hasn't said a word about it. In fact, he's barely said a word at all. He's been coming home late from work, sometimes so late that I'm already in bed. On Thursday night, he didn't come home until well after midnight. The chicken Parma I made him went cold on the bench. My text messages were ignored. I was so upset that I ended up drinking a bottle of wine, then panicked as I calculated how much breast milk I needed to defrost if Mia woke up too early. It was hard to go to mothers' group and not have the same comfortable chit chat and warmth with Marnie. I hadn't known her long, but she's quickly become someone who cares, and I don't have many people like that in my life. But she pissed me off trying to meddle in my relationship, even if she is trying to help. I've ignored her calls for a few days despite desperately needing a friend. Then, when Aaron didn't come home, I opened the bottle of sauv blanc that'd been sitting in the fridge since one of my other failed attempts at a date night with Aaron. When he got home, my head was pounding on the pillow and I didn't acknowledge him.

I gingerly clean my hand with cold water. It stings a little, but it feels good to finally have the sweaty bandage off. I used to treat so many women with injuries like this. They'd come in with bruises, burns and cuts, and repeat rehearsed stories about a staircase or door or unruly dog that tripped them over. I'd listen to them, knowing there was nothing I could do but offer them support in that moment. I wasn't supposed to ask leading questions, and on the few occasions when I pushed the boundaries, my overtures weren't well-received. The hardest part was seeing the same woman return weeks or even days later. I could never understand why they didn't leave. Why would they stay with someone who's putting them in the hospital? But now I get it. Leaving seems so much harder than staying. If I tried to leave Aaron, I'd have no money and nowhere to live. Plus, he'd be so angry. He'd search for us and when he inevitably found us, I'd pay for it.

It's Saturday, so no doubt Aaron will head to the racetrack soon.

'I need the shower,' he says, entering the bathroom.

'Sure. Give me a sec.' I gently towel dry my hand, patting it slowly.

'Bloody hell, can you hurry up? Race one is in thirty minutes.'

My pulse quickens, and my breakfast churns in my stomach. I can't handle another argument right now.

'Sorry.' I rush out of the bathroom and he slams the door before I cross the threshold, the door clipping my heel. I wince. The back of my foot bleeds a little, and I patch it up with a Band-Aid.

When Aaron comes out of the bathroom, I'm preparing some sandwiches and fruit for myself. 'I'm going to sit in the park with Mia today and have a picnic,' I say. 'She'll love laying on the grass in the sun. Do you want to come?'

Aaron makes a face like I've asked the dumbest thing in the world. 'Are you deaf?'

I say nothing.

'Mute now too? I told you race one is starting soon and I need to get to the track.'

'You don't want to spend a day with your daughter and me?'

He laughs and grabs one of the sandwiches from the lunchbox I'd been packing and shoves it into his mouth. 'No thanks,' he says, showing me a mush of Vegemite and bread in his mouth.

My eyes prickle and I work so hard to swallow back the massive sob threatening to escape. Thankfully Mia is asleep, so she doesn't hear this. Even if she's too young to remember, she deserves a dad who wants to spend time with her. Tears spill on to my cheeks and I can no longer hold it together.

'What's your problem?' Aaron says when he notices me crying.

I shake my head. 'Nothing,' I choke out.

He slams his fist on the bench between us. 'What is it?'

'I-I just wish you wanted to spend time with Mia and me.'

'See the food you're making there? See that nice little dress you've got on? How do you think we pay for that?'

I think to myself that bread and Vegemite are mere staples in most households and that this dress is from about six years ago that I re-wear every summer. But I don't dare say it.

'You wouldn't have that if I didn't work. This is my chance to blow off some steam after working my ass off for this family all week.'

I take a deep breath, too scared to say anything.

'Is that okay with you?' he dares me to answer.

I nod.

'And is there anything you want to say?'

I say nothing.

He steps closer. 'Well?'

'Thank you,' I whisper, barely loud enough for him to hear.

'Excuse me?' He grabs my burnt hand and squeezes it. I scream. Bolts of burning pain shoot from my hand up to my shoulder and back again, and it feels like he's scraping my skin with glass. I pull my hand away and put it back under cold water again. I struggle to breathe through the excruciating pain.

Aaron is staring at me, a smirk on his face, still waiting for an answer. I know I should say thank you and leave it. But I'm furious. I'm hurting, physically and emotionally. 'Piss off, Aaron,' I say.

His eyebrows shoot up and he opens his mouth, but nothing comes out. I silently pray that his shock will save me another beating. But he shoves me hard up against the cupboards, knocking the back of my head against the hard timber. Then he grabs his wallet and keys from the table and leaves, slamming the door behind him.

Tears pricking at my eyes, I rub the back of my head before inspecting my hand for the second time this morning. It looks okay but it burns like hell. I dry it off and Mia stirs. I watch her on the monitor for a moment. Beautiful, innocent Mia who has no idea of the family she has been born into. I need to get us out of here.

Chapter 23

Marnie

Rob has been home most of this week thanks to a few rostered days off. Besides cricket training, we've been together the entire time. This was the sort of thing I always longed for when we were trying to get pregnant. I can't call them weekends together because Rob's weekend can fall on any day of the week, but I'd always fantasised about our 'weekends' together as a family. Kids activities, family brunches, bike rides at the park. Obviously, Jasper isn't quite ready to be pedalling around, but quality family time has always been the dream.

However, now that I've got it, it's not living up to my expectations. Rob spends most his time on his phone.

'I'm the boss. The work never stops,' he reminds me each time I sigh at the sound of his phone ringing or alerting him about a message.

And I get it. I do. His work is important. But when he walks out of the room to respond to text messages, I can't help but feel uneasy. I'm sure it's my own insecurities. I don't feel myself, I don't feel attractive and I won't let Rob touch me. Of course, thoughts will race around my head about who he might actually be talking to. I mean, could I blame him if his eyes started to wander?

It's Saturday morning and we plan to get an early breakfast before Rob plays cricket. I'm still in bed, giving Jasper his morning feed. Rob has left the room, once again, to respond to a text message.

'Who was that?' I ask as he comes back in.

He pauses. 'Um, one of the cricket guys asking what time I'm getting to the club this morning.' He throws his phone on the bed and goes in the shower.

I wait for the sound of the water running and the shower door closing. Cradling Jasper against my body, I lean across and grab his phone. I tap the screen and it requests a pin code. My face screws up. That's new. Rob never uses a pin code. I key in his birthday. Incorrect pin. I key in Jasper's birthday, and a photo of Jasper pops up on his home screen. It's one of my favourite pictures of him in blue corduroy overalls that are miles too big for him. My hands are shaking even though I have no real reason to be worried.

Glancing at the closed bathroom door, I bring up Rob's text messages. I can't believe I'm doing this. We've been together for so long and I've never checked up on him. Can I blame the hormones? The most recent text message is from me. That's weird. It's from yesterday afternoon, asking him to bring me a cup of tea while I was feeding Jasper and he was in another room.

I lock his phone again and place it back where he left it. Maybe his cricket mates have a WhatsApp group or Messenger group or something. There are too many avenues for communication these days, and I'm too nervous about getting caught to look through them all. It's Rob. Of course he's telling the truth. I need to snap out of this ridiculous paranoia.

***

'Decaf latte,' the waitress says as she places my coffee in front of me. 'Regular latte,' she adds, and Rob gives her a nod.

'Why are you getting decaf? What's the point?' he asks me.

'I already had a coffee at home.'

'So?'

'So, I don't want to give Jasper any more excuses to not sleep.'

'Don't be ridiculous. Our mums would've had loads of coffee back in the day.'

Back in the day. Is that not the most infuriating phrase that a mother hears? *Back in the day, I ate loads of soft cheese while I was pregnant. It was fine to have a wine or two back in the day. When you were a baby, I put blankets and toys in your cot.*

I'm instantly taken back to the painful years of trying to fall pregnant. The advice Rob's mum, and even my mum, would give me on foods to eat, how to track my ovulation the 'good old-fashioned way' and what positions we should try. *Gross!* I swear we tried everything. I was peeing on sticks constantly, and each month half of our grocery bill went to ovulation tests, pregnancy tests and then, devastatingly, tampons and a butt-load of ice cream. It was a relief when we finally agreed to go down the IVF road. It wasn't just our problem anymore; we had experts to help us. The endless injections, the money, the heartache when it doesn't work, the hormones. My gosh, the hormones. I think I cried nearly every day for two years.

Anyway, it's bad enough when my mother or in-laws go down the *Back in the day* line of conversation, but when my husband joins the chorus, I want to throw my decaf latte in his ignorant face.

Instead, I sip my coffee and ignore him. He'll be at cricket when I'm dealing with a restless baby in a few hours. Maybe it's not the caffeine, but most parents are going to try every damn thing they can to make their baby sleep for a few minutes longer.

'Have you heard from Fleur lately?' he asks, changing the subject.

I shake my head. 'She isn't returning my calls or replying to my texts.' A fact that makes me feel sick. I'm constantly paranoid about whether she's okay.

'You should've left it like I said to.'

Rolling my eyes, I respond, 'I don't need an *I told you so* lecture. I'm worried about her.'

He takes my hand from across the table. 'I'm sorry. I know you are. But there's nothing you can do. These women, it's awful. They often take a long time to accept help and try to leave. I've seen it many times before.'

'How can you switch off from that?'

'I don't. I think about every woman and child I haven't been able to help. They haunt my thoughts every night. All you can do is remind Fleur that you're there for her.'

'I'll text her again later.'

'I need to head off shortly,' Rob says.

I check my watch. 'Jasper will wake from his nap soon.' He's been sleeping in the pram like a champion this morning. See, why would I want to ruin that with coffee? 'Maybe once I've fed him, we'll come down and watch.' I used to watch Rob play cricket most weekends when we lived in the city. I had a great group of girls that I'd go with. We called ourselves the WAGS, and we'd make platters and take cooler bags with wine to the matches. Every Saturday was a mini event. I haven't been to a match since we moved here. Partly because we have Jasper now, but also because I don't know anyone and I feel too old and too boring to meet people.

Rob rubs at the stubble on his chin. 'Oh, that's okay. You don't have to come down. It's warm. Jasper will get irritable.'

'I want to come though. And Jasper's going to have to get used to spending his Saturdays at the club.'

He continues to rub at his face. 'Sure. I guess he will.'

'I'll see how he is after his feed and I'll let you know.'

Rob leaves and I ponder another day of motherhood monotony.

Chapter 24

Peyton

Lucas wakes up so much better this morning. It's been so awful listening to his breathing the last few nights, but he bounced back so quickly.

'Breast milk is wonderful stuff,' Mum says when she takes him from me so I can have breakfast.

I roll my eyes, much the same way as I did when Zara said the same thing in the group message. Mum knows I'd much rather give Lucas formula, so I can have my boobs back and leave the house without the risk of springing a leak. She constantly drops hints about the benefits of breastfeeding, and this is another 'told you so' moment.

'What are you guys going to do today now he's feeling better? It's a beautiful weekend.'

I hadn't even thought about it. Weekend, weekday, it's all the same. I know what I'd like to do, or more to the point, who I'd like to do, but that won't happen.

I shrug.

'Well, what about your mothers' group friends? Or Bree?' she asks. 'Maybe you could do something with them?'

'They all have partners, Mum. I'm sure they're doing family stuff. And Bree will be at the club. I can't take Lucas there.'

'Of course you can.'

I shake my head. 'Half the guys down there don't even know I have a baby. I don't want to deal with all the questions about who the father is or the lectures about how young I am.'

I've known most of those guys my whole life. I'm not in the mood to hear about how I've ruined my life and be asked what I'm going to do for money or how I'll ever buy a house.

Mum's expression softens. 'One day, you're going to have to face it, you know?' She smiles down at Lucas. 'But remember, whatever they say, all that matters is that you have a beautiful, healthy little boy who we all love.'

I sigh. She's right. But I'm not ready for that yet. Plus, I don't want Rob knowing.

'Look,' Mum continues. 'I'll take care of Lucas this afternoon and you go hang out with Bree. We can work towards Lucas' cricket club debut.' She laughs at herself.

'Really?'

'Yep, go for it. Your dad's out, anyway. Lucas will be good company.' She bops Lucas on the nose. 'Won't you?' He smiles up at her, and there's that stirring of jealousy and guilt at war with the desire to feel and act nineteen again.

'Thanks Mum.'

***

There's a flutter in my stomach as I walk to the club. It's a shame I have to be home for dinner, but Lakesfield are playing against the bottom of the table today so with a bit of luck it might wrap up early, and I can have a quick drink with the team. With Rob.

'They're making fast work of it.' Bree gives me a rundown of the morning when I arrive. 'Only chasing a hundred and five runs, and Jonesy's already on thirty-five.'

My breath hitches at the mention of Rob, even though I hate hearing his nickname coming out of Bree's mouth. I smile. 'Awesome.' Not that I care about the team doing well. Just that it'll be over in the next hour and then I can speak to him.

My prediction ends up being a little off. Rob loses his wicket not long after I arrive, and then we lose a few more quickly. It takes almost two hours. Lots of safe, boring blocking, but the boys get the win well before I need to head off.

The crowd of spectators slowly shuffles inside, buying drinks and snacks. The team is downstairs in the change rooms doing whatever guys do in cricket team change rooms. In my head, it's like a locker room scene from *Top Gun*—Dad's favourite movie—and despite Tom Cruise being way too old and weird, I can't deny his body is hot. An image that immediately takes me back to Rob taking his shirt off on my couch last Saturday. My skin tingles.

'Drink?' Bree asks, snapping me out of my daydream.

'Yes please!' I reach for my purse.

'Don't worry, you get the next one. Meet you outside.'

I grab a table outside and look around, trying not to look as though I'm staring at the stairs that lead down to the change rooms.

Now I don't know how to classify me and Rob in terms of our relationship—casually dating, summer fling, booty call? I don't know. But we text, we've hooked up, he's been to my house—surely that warrants a hello? When Rob comes upstairs, he sees me, and rather than joy or lust or excitement, his face spells panic. His eyes widen and then narrow and his head tilts, as though he's trying to work out a puzzle. I smile and wave him over. He puts up a finger as if to say wait and then walks away and pulls out his phone. I glance down at my phone, thinking he might be texting me, but nothing comes through.

I can't deny that I'm disappointed. I look hot today in a short denim skirt and white crop that shows off a hint of my abs beneath. Whatever. His loss. I walk up to some of his teammates and start chatting with them. They're old friends of my brothers, but a little harmless flirting won't hurt, and hopefully it'll remind Rob what he's missing out on.

I laugh loudly at one of the guy's jokes and gently shove him. 'Stop,' I say, as though whatever he's saying is too funny. Then I turn to see Rob walking over to the group. *Men. So bloody predictable.*

'Hey Peyt,' Rob says and joins in the conversation with the group.

I give him a quick nod. 'I need a refill.' Bypassing Bree to get her order, I go to the bar.

'Two ciders please, Jake.'

Jake returns to the counter with two glasses.

'I'll get them,' a voice says from behind me. It's Rob.

'These are for Bree and me,' I say. I don't want him thinking I've gone to buy him a drink when I'm trying to play hard to get.

'That's okay. Make it one more mate,' he says to Jake. 'Can we go outside?' he asks as we leave the bar.

'Sure.' I deliver Bree's drink and follow him out to the balcony. 'What's up?'

'Look, sorry for ignoring you before. I was waiting for an important message. Anyway, I'm allowed to talk to you now.'

'*Allowed* to talk to me?' My face scrunches up. What does he mean?

'Oh, as in now I can talk to you without getting distracted.' He sounds flustered.

I shrug. Whatever. He's talking to me now. That's all I care about.

'Jonesy, do you want a drink?' one of the other players says, approaching the two of us.

'I'm good mate, thanks.'

'What about your Mrs?'

Rob flushes and then says a little too quickly. 'Not my Mrs. Um, drink?' he asks, turning to me.

I shake my head, and the guy leaves.

'I don't think you could've answered that quicker if you tried.' I say, laughing as I do to make it seem like I'm joking and not completely offended.

'Sorry,' he says. Then he leans in closer and whispers. 'No labels are more fun.' His warm breath in my ear makes me shiver.

I desperately wish we weren't in a public place, or that it was dark so we could sneak out to the carpark. My breathing gets heavier as we stare at each other.

Then his lips are at my ear again, brushing it ever so slightly, and I close my eyes.

'Meet me downstairs in a minute,' he says and walks away.

The changerooms stink like body odour combined with deodorant and sports gel. But I'm not fussy. Not when the man in front of me already has his shirt off, his abs begging me to run my hands over them.

Rob pulls me into him and kisses my neck slowly, working his way down. He slips the thin strap of my dress from my shoulder and keeps going. I sigh loudly and press myself against him. Neither of us hold back.

I don't think the *Top Gun* scene will be what pops into my head when I think of change rooms anymore. It'll be the way Rob held me against the lockers and reminded me how well he can move. I return to the clubhouse a few minutes before Rob.

We spend the next hour chatting and whispering more things we want to do to each other. When Mum texts me for the third time in fifteen minutes, I snap out of the fantasy and sigh as I pick up the phone. Each message seems more annoyed than the previous one and I can imagine Mum's pissed off pursed lips as she taps away at her phone, tutting at nobody.

> *Just checking how far away you are?*

> *Peyt, have you left yet?*

> *You said you'd be home by 5:30 Peyton. It's 6. Have you forgotten you have a son?*

I shield my phone up toward me, hoping that Rob hasn't seen the messages. It's embarrassing enough being nagged to come home by my mum, but I don't want him to know I have a kid.

'I have to go.' Sighing, I throw my head back dramatically, as if this is the worst thing to ever happen to me.

Rob laughs. 'I have to get home too.' He checks his watch. 'Shit, like now.'

I don't know what he's in a rush for, but I don't get a chance to ask.

'See ya babe,' he says, and he pecks me on the cheek in the same way you greet a friend, then rushes off.

It's not like I want to make a scene at the cricket club by having a full on pash, but he could've at least walked me out and given me something a little spicier around the corner. I walk home and brace myself for Mum's next lecture.

Chapter 25

Amalia

When Marnie texted the group asking who was free for a drink tonight, I wasn't sure how to respond, especially since no one else was available. I'd decided to avoid the cricket club earlier today because I didn't want to see Rob or Peyton, or worse, both of them together. I also wasn't super keen on hanging out with his wife and pretending that everything was okay. But she'd seemed so excited in her messages about having a night off and pumping some milk so she could enjoy some drinks, and I didn't have the heart to say no.

Unfortunately, Mrs Casci had already made plans when I'd told her I wasn't going out earlier, so Marnie said she'd come to my place instead. Tidying up my tiny two-bedroom townhouse, I picture Marnie's beautiful house on the other side of town and my cheeks redden, wondering what she'll think when she sees my dull kitchen and the browning tiles in my bathroom.

When the doorbell rings I'm so nervous that my stomach turns and my mouth fills with saliva. How ridiculous. Marnie's lovely. But it's what she possibly represents that scares me. What if she lets me down like Marcus and Kya did?

I open the door and Marnie smiles. 'Sorry I'm a bit late. Rob got back from the club late. Apparently the match went longer than expected.'

Lie. I'd already spoken to Kya who'd been drinking with the team since like three o'clock.

'That's okay, come in. Excuse the mess.'

There's literally no mess because I've cleaned everything from top to bottom, but I feel like everyone says that when they have people over. She hands me a bottle of wine, and I lead her to the kitchen to get some glasses.

'Cheers,' she says, clinking her glass against mine before taking a big swig of pinot noir. She nods to herself, looking at her glass, as though pleased with her wine selection.

'Cheers,' I reply. When the wine hits my lips, it relaxes me instantly. It's delicious and familiar, and I'm beginning to feel excited. Could this be the start of something? 'How'd you get the night off?' I take another big sip.

'I had a rough day with Jasper. He was not interested in sleep this afternoon.'

I nod, totally getting it. Gone are the days when our newborn blobs slept for hours on end. Gone are those peaceful little bundles we had to wake to feed. Now they need an endless amount of shushing and rocking and patting and why has no one invented an impossible-to-spit-out dummy?

'Anyway,' Marnie continues. 'I'd hoped to get down to the club to watch Rob play.'

My heart skips a beat. Marnie can't go there. 'Really?' I ask, trying to sound like that'd be the worst thing to do.

'I know, I know. People think cricket is boring, but I've always gone to his games, and I haven't even been to his new club.'

Thank goodness.

'So I texted Rob this arvo and said that I wouldn't make it, but that I'd love a night to myself. He came straight home and here I am.' She lifts her glass completely unaware that her scumbag husband didn't go straight home.

'Nice,' I lie. 'So what do you want to do? Movie?' I feel like I'd probably fall asleep if I put a movie on, but I'm also out of practise when it comes to entertaining.

'Yeah alright. Something light. I don't think I have the brain capacity for anything too hectic.'

We agree on a classic romcom, *How to Lose a Guy in 10 Days*, and get comfortable on the couch with our wines. I keep the volume low because I don't want to wake Lila but also because then we can still chat but without the awkward silences in between.

The scene plays where Kate Hudson's character, Andie, is at couple's counselling with Matthew McConaughey's character, Ben, who has no idea it's a fake session run by Andie's friend.

'Do you think couple's counselling works?' Marnie asks. 'I mean not the fake type they're doing but, you know, actual couple's counselling?'

I wasn't expecting the question, and there's a flutter of panic in me. I'm not sure how to answer, especially given I haven't been in a relationship where I've contemplated therapy. When things get hard, it's 'see ya later'.

'Not sure. Don't know anyone who's been.'

Marnie watches the scene play out, engrossed in what happens during the fake session. It's hilarious, actually. Kate Hudson plays crazy so well.

'Why?' I ask.

She sighs. 'I don't know. Sometimes I wonder if it may be worth Rob and I giving it a try. We've been together so long and been through so much that I worry we're drifting apart.'

She's openly admitting to me that her marriage isn't super healthy, and that she wants to fix it, while I sit here knowing it's probably beyond repair. Shit, I'm a bad person for saying nothing. Instead, I say, 'Well, maybe talk to him about it. See if he'd be willing to go.'

She shrugs. 'Yeah maybe.'

On the screen, Ben has worked out his whole family is helping Andie beat him at Bullshit. As he throws his cards down and the family laughs, there's a bang on the door, and we both jump.

'Amalia, open up.'

My stomach drops, and the heat drains from my face. It's Marcus.

'Is everything okay?' Marnie asks. 'Who's that?'

I exhale loudly. 'That's Lila's dad, Marcus. He often comes around unannounced. Either to see Lila or, um, to see me. He can be quite persistent.'

Marnie looks at the door and then back at me.

'I can't deal with him right now,' I say, exhaling loudly.

Marnie's eyes narrow. 'Want me to ask him to leave?' And she marches over.

I quickly jump between her and the door. 'No, don't. It's not worth it.' I've told him where to go a thousand times before but he never listens. Marnie saying it would make him angrier.

'I can hear you in there. Open up!' he shouts.

My body tenses. He seems to be getting more aggressive every time I see him.

Marnie gives me a look that shows her age; wise, sensible, and, somehow, sober. I step aside. She opens the door.

'Who the hell are you?' he shouts.

I'm shocked at the way he yells. Then the scent of bourbon hits me, and it makes more sense. Still, Marcus has never been one to raise his voice. Not until recently.

Marnie instinctively takes a step back. 'I'm a friend of Amalia's. We're in the middle of a movie. Can she call you when it's a good time for you to visit?'

Marcus looks at me and then back at Marnie before bursting out laughing. 'Is she serious?'

'Marcus, please. Come back to see Lila another time. I'm busy tonight.' I hate myself. Why do I do this? Why am I telling him to come another time? It's asking for trouble.

'You can't stop me from seeing my daughter.' He tries to move past Marnie, but she puts her arm out. His face reddens and sweat beads at his temples. 'Move.' His tone makes me shiver.

'Marnie, it's fine,' I say.

She turns to me. 'No, it's not.' Marnie keeps her arm out, hand firmly pressed against the door frame, and she looks back to Marcus. 'Amalia has asked you to leave. My husband is a cop, and he can be here in minutes if I need him to be.'

I close my eyes. I don't want to see his reaction to that. Before he cheated, he was my best friend. I thought we'd be together forever. When we found out we were pregnant, he was so excited and loved picking things for the nursery. I still care about him.

There are some grunts and footsteps before the door clicks closed.

'It's okay, Amalia, he's gone.'

I open my eyes and Marnie is standing in front of me, placing her hands on my shoulders. I blink back tears.

'I think you should come and speak to Rob about him. He seems dangerous. He might be able to help.'

I nod, even though there's absolutely no way I'll be doing that. 'Thank you.' He's never laid a finger on me. But tonight, he scared me. I know he's hurting, but there's no excuse for what just happened.

We watch the rest of the movie. We've well and truly sobered up. The jokes are less funny, and the romance is nauseating. Marnie leaves, but not before putting Rob's number in my phone and giving me a stern warning to lock the door.

I get into bed and I'm somewhat relieved and happy that Marnie must care for me. It feels amazing to be protected and supported like that. This is what my mum had. I get it now.

Then my phone buzzes. It's Marcus.

`I'll be back.`

I need a plan. I need him out of my life.

Chapter 26

Marnie

After enjoying a night off from feeding and shushing and rocking on Saturday, I'm feeling somewhat human again. A little rested. My bucket is a little fuller. Rob had to work the night shift on Sunday but was home Monday, and we had a nice, quiet family day. He's been better with his phone. I haven't looked at it again, as much as I've wanted to. I'm trying to remind myself that he's the new sergeant in town and lots of different people need him.

Last night Fleur texted me asking to walk today. It's Tuesday and Rob is back at work, so I agree, despite us not speaking for over a week. It seems I'm becoming the go-to friend for these poor women, and it's challenging for me, exhausting. Back when I was teaching in the city, we had to do online courses every year about mandatory reporting of abuse. We were taught the signs of emotional, physical and sexual abuse and shown how to report it. It was a sad reality of our job, and I had to make several reports in my fifteen years of teaching. Sometimes the police would come, once even Rob came to my school. So, reporting this sort of thing was my job, and there would've been serious repercussions for me if I hadn't done it. Thinking about how Fleur is possibly being treated and seeing Amalia's ex last night and not being able to do anything about any of it is horrible. But they're not my students, they're my friends. They're not kids, they're adults. I can only support them.

I arrive at the park before Fleur. I'm chuffed with myself as she pushes Mia towards me.

'Check me out,' I say, 'I'm early and my hair is washed!' Although, it's not lost on me that her hair is styled beautifully, as always.

She laughs. 'That's quite the achievement.'

'Rob's been home for a few days, and Jasper slept through for the first time. I woke up feeling like a new woman.'

She looks into the pram. 'Great job, little man! Keep it up for your mama.'

We begin what's becoming our regular route around the park. The conversation starts off superficial and awkward.

After a long silence, I stop and turn to her. 'Fleur, I'm so sorry. It's none of my business what happens between you and Aaron. I should've never said anything.'

I look into her sad eyes and then her tears spill over. We pull the prams over to a bench and take a seat. I hand her a tissue and put my arms around her.

Chapter 27

Fleur

I sit there in Marnie's embrace and cry. I don't know how long we sit like that, but Mia starts to cry, and I pull myself together.

'Think I might feed her here,' I say, lifting her from the pram.

I wasn't prepared for a public feed, so I have to pull my t-shirt right up to get access to my bra.

Marnie gasps. 'What the hell, Fleur?'

Shit. I'd forgotten about the fresh bruises on my ribs from the weekend.

I hesitate. 'Oh that,' I fake a laugh. 'Let's just say that after almost a year of not drinking, I wasn't great at handling the stairs at home.'

Marnie isn't an idiot. As if she's going to believe the old 'I fell down the stairs' excuse. I don't even have stairs. I look down at Mia and pretend to help her latch, hoping to avoid showing my reddening cheeks.

'That seems like quite a nasty fall. Have you had it checked? You could have a broken rib.'

'Oh nah. It's fine.'

'I know you were a nurse, but you don't have x-ray vision.'

'Aaron would be furious if I saw a doctor.'

The words are out of my mouth before I even have a chance to think. That's it. I've done it. I've screwed up everything. Looking away from Marnie, I stare at nothing in particular, wishing I'd never gone out today.

'Fleur.' Her voice is gentle and she places a hand on my knee. 'Why would Aaron be furious?'

The tears fall again, and I realise I can't hide it. I'm all out of excuses for him. It's time to admit there's a problem. 'He'd be angry because he gave me these bruises.'

I take a deep breath. It's done. The truth is out. I feel relieved and completely terrified. I'd thought about telling someone since that first time he hit me. The night of my birthday. The night I forgot to remind him of my birthday. The blow had come hard and fast into the ribs. I can't remember crying. I'd been completely and utterly shocked. The bruise that developed over the following days was huge and dark, and I worried constantly about someone seeing it despite it being in such a carefully chosen place on Aaron's part.

Now it's finally out there. Someone else finally knows. It feels as though Marnie has lifted a hundred kilos of painful weight off my shoulders.

I continue. 'Rob came over again on Sunday. Another noise complaint. Aaron thinks I've been blabbing to you at mothers' group, ironic right? And he's angry that Rob's being nosey, so he pushed me.'

'Fleur, I'm so sorry. I feel like this is my fault.'

I laugh. A manic sort of laugh because I don't know how to feel. 'Don't feel bad. He was doing this long before you and Rob showed up.'

'And your hand?' she asks.

I lift my hand, now bandage-free but still red. 'He hit me with the iron.'

Marnie is the one in tears now. 'I can't believe someone could do this. Fleur, you have to speak to Rob or someone else at the station. They can help you.'

'I can't. I have nothing without Aaron.'

'You'll end up dead if you stay there, and then Mia will have nothing.'

The thought hits me like a freight train. If I wasn't here to protect and care for Mia, who would? A violent, drunken gambler?

I look down at my beautiful girl, blissfully unaware as she suckles away.

'Will you help me?'

Marnie puts an arm around me and with tears running down both of our faces, she says, 'Of course.'

Chapter 28

Marnie

It's been a few days since my walk with Fleur and haven't been able to stop thinking about her. Her bruised body occupies my nightmares, and my mind always races to the worst-case scenario. She isn't responding to my texts, and I know Rob would be furious if I went around there. He's acting strange enough without me pissing him off too. He's working longer hours and at the cricket club a lot, and when he's home, he's either sleeping or texting. I'm in a rut, waiting to feel myself again, waiting for my marriage to return to normal, but if anything, things seem to be getting worse.

It's Thursday, mothers' group day, and I'm relieved I'll see Fleur, but I can't help myself—I have to stop by the accounting agency where Aaron works first. I figure it's a public setting. *What's the worst that could happen?*

I park the car outside the community centre because the company he works for is at the end of the strip anyway, and I'll do anything to avoid the whole pram set up-pack down routine any more than necessary. The car park is empty. I'm relieved because I wasn't sure how I'd explain this to Fleur if she happened to be here early.

I know the office I'm looking for because I've been to the cute little gift shop next door with Rob a few times. It's the kind that sells the most gorgeous little gift cards for astronomical prices, and yet I have a pile of them at home for no event, just in case. They also sell adorable baby things like bibs and burp cloths. I could get the same in a department store for half the price, but the prints there are so adorable.

I stop by the store and do a quick lap, willing myself to not pick up any items, to leave the shop without buying anything. But then I spy the cutest mug, and I can't go past it. I've always teased Rob for being a typical cop who loves his donuts. I always thought it was a stereotype or a thing in the movies, but one lady who worked with him in Melbourne brought donuts into work every day, and his addiction stuck. The mug has a big strawberry donut printed on it with red love-heart-shaped sprinkles. Below it in black text it says: Donut go breaking my heart. '*Don't go breaking my heart*' was our go to karaoke song back in our younger days. I have to buy it.

After handing over far more cash than necessary for a novelty mug, I slowly walk to the accounting office. I push the door open with my butt while pulling the pram in, catching a wheel on the door frame. You need a license for these things.

An older lady sits behind a desk and peers over her glasses at us, looking amused.

'Can I help you?' she asks.

'Hi, yes. Um, I was wondering if Aaron is here.'

'Do you have an appointment?'

I shake my head and look down at Jasper, hoping it might buy me some sympathy.

'You really need an appointment,' she says, looking down at Jasper, who has now got a sock in his mouth. 'But since you've clearly got your hands full, I'll see if he's available now.'

'Thank you so much.'

A few minutes later, a tall man walks into the entrance area. He looks as though he could be attractive with long, thick hair, blue eyes and a sharp jawline. But his hair is slicked back with little care and he has black bags below his red-rimmed eyes.

He looks at me and smiles. 'Hi, you asked to see me?'

'Yes, I won't take too much time. Is there somewhere we can talk privately?'

From the corner of my eye, I see the receptionist glare at me.

'Follow me,' he says and leads me into an office.

He closes the door and sits behind a large desk. I stay standing near the door, suddenly wondering what the hell I'm doing here and why on earth I'd bring Jasper with me. But then the same images that have haunted my dreams for the past few days flash through my mind again, and I know I have to say it.

'I'm a friend of your wife, Fleur.'

A flash of panic crosses his eyes, and then it's gone. 'Oh good. I've been hoping she'd make some friends in town. She misses Melbourne.'

'Yeah she does. She misses a lot of things about Melbourne.'

He leans forward in his seat and lowers his voice. 'Is there a reason you're here?'

'I've seen the bruises on Fleur's body. My husband is a police officer.' I try to keep my voice from shaking. I can't believe I'm doing something so stupid. Rob will be furious. 'Keep your hands off her, or he'll be paying you another visit.'

Aaron is out of his seat in a second, crossing the room quickly. 'So your husband is that cop that showed up?' His face is so close to mine now. He plants a hand on the door behind me. His arm is skimming my cheek and I can smell the stale alcohol on his breath. 'You and your pig husband can mind your own damn business.'

Jasper is in the pram beside me, staring up. I'm grateful he'll never remember this moment. He moves another step closer so that his body is pressed against mine. Then he knees me hard in the thigh, and I crumble to the floor. He drags me up by the arm and pulls me away from the door. I lunge for the pram, and he opens the door.

'It was lovely to meet you,' he says loudly, no doubt for the receptionist's benefit. 'See you again soon.'

My breathing has only just settled when I hobble up to the community centre. My thigh hurts a lot. I'm glad I wore leggings today because I'm certain a bruise is already making an appearance. As I arrive, Peyton, Fleur and Hanbi are out the front talking. Mothers' group is a weird phenomenon. A group of random women thrown together based purely on the date of birth of their first child and their local area. They're asked to share personal things with each other and bond over their entry into motherhood. I'd have never met these women, let alone befriend them, if it weren't for this group. But over the last few weeks, I've formed friendships, some closer than others, and some that'll probably last as our children grow up together. I hear them laughing as I get closer to the group. Hanbi and Peyton smile at me and keep chatting. Fleur looks down at Mia, avoiding eye contact with me.

'What's so funny?' I ask, trying to join in the conversation. Trying to feel like I'm back in Melbourne with my girlfriends. Trying to forget I was assaulted by Fleur's husband.

Hanbi giggles. A school girl giggle that does not suit her professional, working mum persona. 'Peyton was telling us about a guy she's met at the cricket club. The one she, you know.' Hanbi winks and then looks at Peyton. 'Oh to be young again,' she says in a sing-song voice.

Peyton rolls her eyes. 'Can you stop?'

My heart races. The cricket club. There's only one club in town. It has to be the same one. But there's lots of guys around a cricket club, players and coaches and the ones that enjoy the cheap booze and banter. I can't shake the funny feeling though.

'I thought I could hear you lot gasbagging out here.' Liz pops her head out the door before I get a chance to ask Peyton any questions. 'Come inside. The others are here.'

Zara and Amalia are already sitting in the circle. There's no point trying to strategically choose a spot any more to avoid going first. Liz picks on anyone. I take an empty seat next to Zara. Fleur ignores the seat next to me to sit on the other side of Zara.

'Today we will discuss baby health and creating a safe home environment.'

I'm already dreading it. Even though I want to know everything I should be doing, I find it so overwhelming and the consequences are terrifying.

'Our session will be a little different today. We won't go around the circle sharing. Instead, I'll run through some important things to consider and then let you ask any questions.'

The room relaxes. The pressure is off. Zara straightens in her chair, far too keen. I can only imagine how safe, clean and perfect her home is. She frustrates me, but I know it's because I wish I was a little more like her, more kept together.

Liz continues, 'Let's start with safe sleeping.'

After ten minutes of non-stop speaking on Liz's part, my brain is overloaded, and I wish I'd been taking notes. Childproofing the home, transitioning safely to a cot, raising children with pets, water safety and first aid—there's so much to think about. I count the breaths in my head as I look at Jasper sleeping silently in my arms. Every part of me wishes so desperately to keep him safe and healthy. My anxiety heightens and my usual ticks are hard to hide—biting my nails and twirling my hair. I can't keep still. Thankfully Liz asks for questions or comments so the others can draw any attention away from me.

'So,' Zara begins, and I already want to roll my eyes. 'We won't be moving Tiana from our room until after the recommended six months.'

Of course she won't be. Rob and I have already talked about moving Jasper. We need sleep. And maybe it'll help with some other things in the bedroom too.

'We also did a baby first aid course and childproofed the house and yard.'

'Are you serious?' Hanbi says. My cheeks burn thinking about the premature baby proofing I've already done. 'Your kid can't even move yet. What could you possibly need to have done already?'

'It's never too early to put your child's safety first.' Zara's tone is too sweet, so condescending.

'It's okay. You have time to get organised, and perhaps Zara will share some things she's done around the house,' Liz says.

I know Liz is trying to defuse the situation, but she didn't need to encourage her to keep going. We listen to Zara list a range of supplies she recommends from the hardware store before getting into a conversation about pets.

Fleur hasn't said a word for the entire session, and I think about the safety situation—or lack thereof—in her home. The conversation and questions are beginning to wrap up, and I can't help myself, I have to say something. 'Um, Liz, I'm wondering what support there is out there for victims of domestic violence.'

Fleur glares at me, her eyes burning into me with pure anger. The rest of the mums look at me concerned. Zara even gasps, clapping her hand to her mouth.

'Oh no, no, sorry, not me. My husband's a police officer, and I know he sees this kind of thing. I'd like to know if there's support for mums and kids in these situations?'

Fleur stands up. 'Poop explosion.' She rushes for the exit, despite there being a change table in the bathroom.

'Good question, Marnie. I've got some flyers in the office. I'll get them now.'

Liz leaves the room, and the rest of us sit in silence.

Chapter 29

Amalia

It's only Marnie, Peyton and I at the surf club for a drink after our session today. Fleur raced out of the community centre faster than I thought humanly possible when lugging a pram. Hanbi went back to work, and Zara straight up said she didn't want to come. Zara and Hanbi clashed during the session, but it wasn't the first time. Besides Hanbi wasn't even coming. Perhaps Zara felt the tension which often arose after one of her comments. It's not that I don't think she is doing a great job, and I'm sure everything she said is true, but it's the way she says things that puts my back up. It's as though she thinks she is better than the rest of us. Her absence certainly isn't going to bother me.

'Hopefully that guy isn't working today,' I say, referring to Peyton's old schoolmate, as we walk over the road to the club. I'm pleased with myself for starting the conversation.

'Gosh, I hope not. But I'm sure he'll avoid me if he is. Teen mums repel young guys.'

'Sounds like you don't repel all guys though,' Marnie says.

Oh shit. Oh shit. Oh shit. I don't like where this is going.

'I said young guys,' Peyton says and laughs. 'Plus he doesn't know I'm a mum.'

'Does anyone know what's wrong with Fleur?' I cut off the conversation before it goes too far.

We walk to a table out on the balcony, parking our prams awkwardly. At least there are only three prams to fit in this time.

'She said poop explosion,' Marnie says.

'Yeah but there's a change table there. She didn't have to run away,' Peyton says.

Marnie shrugs. 'Maybe she didn't have extra clothes for Mia or something.'

'It was weird,' Peyton responds.

An older woman comes over to take our order, and we decide on another bottle of wine.

'Have you heard any more from Marcus?' Marnie asks, turning to me.

I look to Peyton. I haven't told her about my situation. Marnie dumped me in it. I want to be annoyed, but at the same time, maybe she's doing me a favour. I want to be close to these women. And it's better than discussing Peyton's love life.

'Thankfully, no. He texted me after you left on Saturday saying he'd be back, but he hasn't dropped by.'

'What's going on?' Peyton asks, pouring the wine that's been placed on the table. 'Who's Marcus?'

'Marcus is Lila's father. We were together for a while. He cheated on me while I was pregnant. I want him out of my life but he's threatening to get lawyers involved if I don't let him see Lil.'

Peyton's eyes widen. 'Whoa. Okay.' She hands me a glass. 'Here, you need this.'

I take a sip.

'Anyway, he's harmless,' I add.

'Didn't seem that way on Saturday,' Marnie says.

'He'd had a bit to drink. He never usually raises his voice like that.'

'That's how it starts. I hear about it all the time. Remember what I told you.'

This conversation is heading dangerously close to Rob territory again. Why does it have to be just these two at drinks today? Even one other person would take the heat off me steering this conversation constantly away from the mention of Rob or the cricket club or the fact he's a cop.

'I know, I know. All good,' I take another large sip of my wine. 'Do you think Zara will ever join us for a drink again?'

'Hope not!' Peyton says. Then she shakes her head. 'Sorry, that was so bitchy. She makes me feel so bad about myself. I hate breastfeeding. Surely, I'm not the only one.'

'Some days I love it, some days I hate it,' Marnie says. 'She's lovely. But she's full on.'

I smile. Crisis averted, again.

We finish the bottle of wine, chatting mostly about formula brands and which sterilisers we use. I haven't explored formula feeding yet, but I am making note of their suggestions.

'Alright mums, I'm out of here,' Peyton says. 'I'm going out later.'

'Where are you going?' Marnie asks.

Thursday night. I know exactly where she's going. Come on, universe. I've made it through an hour with these two women and managed to avoid the topic. Don't let me down now.

Jasper lets out a loud screeching sound, and I almost burst out laughing. Surely that wasn't the universe. Nevertheless, I'm grateful because it distracts Marnie, and we're all out the door and saying our goodbyes without continuing the conversation.

Chapter 30

Peyton

'Four down, one to go! You proud, Mum?' I say, walking in after mothers' group.

'Peyt, it's not meant to be a chore that you countdown to finishing,' Mum says. 'I thought you were getting on well with some of the other mums.'

It wasn't a chore at all. I was genuinely enjoying Thursdays now, mainly the wine part. But every so often I'm reminded that I'm much younger than them, and I'm doing different things with my life. Sometimes I feel like I have nothing in common with them besides our babies ages and our postcode. But we do have a laugh. And they are super supportive.

'Yeah, I am. The sessions are a little lame though.' It's not entirely a lie.

'Are you going to the club tonight?'

I've been looking forward to this all week, especially since I couldn't get out last Thursday.

'If that's okay with you?'

'Yep.' Mum takes Lucas from my arms. 'Are we going to have a Grandma-Lucas night, little man?' she says in a gushing voice up close to his face.

Lucas gives her a big smile. I wish I had that bond with him. I wonder if I'll ever have that maternal side that is so natural to Mum.

***

'You left early on Saturday,' Bree says, pulling up a chair at the table outside.

'Yeah, Mum was on my back about getting home to Lucas.'

'Ahh, fair enough,' Bree responds before taking a big sip of her cocktail, and selfishly it annoys me because she has no idea about responsibility.

I settle into my usual habit of people watching and sipping cider. Bree chats to some guys who are at our table, and I'm thankful they're there, so I don't have to listen to her.

My phone buzzes. Rob's out in the carpark. My heart races. But why do we have to keep sneaking around in the carpark? I mean, I don't want to grind up on him in front of a crowd, but he's allowed to come talk to me, flirt with me, surely.

I head outside. The sun hasn't completely set yet, so there's enough light to spot Rob's car at the back of the car park.

'Why aren't you coming inside for a drink?'

Rob's leaning against the back of his car, looking out over one of the ovals. 'I can't stay long tonight, so I wanted to prioritise my time.' His smile is mischievous, and it takes all my willpower to not jump him straight away.

'You're allowed to talk to me inside, you know?' I say, edging close to him.

'I know. But then I wouldn't be able to do this.'

He hooks his arm around my waist and pulls me in, his lips millimetres from mine.

'Well, you could,' I say breathily. 'But the guys are mates with my brother, so good move on your part.'

His mouth is on mine, fast and eager at first, and then slow. His hand traces down my back to my waist and pulls me closer still.

And then his phone rings. He lets out a frustrated groan.

'Ignore it,' I plead, pulling his face back down to meet mine.

'It could be work.' He puts his hand in his pocket, clearly frustrated, and drops his phone. The screen lights up and a familiar face looks up at me from the ground.

'What the hell?' My stomach drops. I bend down to pick his phone up before he can. 'Who's this?'

Then it all starts to make sense. Marnie. *My husband is a police officer.* Acting weird when I mentioned the cricket club. And Rob, always sneaking around or never replying.

'Who's this?' I say, louder this time and slamming his phone against his chest.

He looks guilty as hell. 'I've been meaning to tell you. I have a son.'

'Jasper is *your* son?' My skin is crawling.

Rob's face pales. 'You know Jasper?'

'Jasper is two weeks younger than my son, Lucas. We're in the same mothers' group...me and your *wife.*'

'You have a son?'

'*That's* your response?' I'm yelling now. 'You're married!'

Rob grabs me by the shoulders. 'Peyton, stop yelling. People are going to hear you.'

'Hear what! That you're a lying, cheating dirtbag?'

'I didn't mean for this to happen. Things have been so weird with Marns and me, and then you came along, and I felt wanted again.'

'What? So, I'm just here to stroke your ego while your wife sits at home with your son. You asshole!'

I storm off back towards the clubhouse. Rob calls out behind me but doesn't follow. Tears start to fall. I'm so angry. Angry for being used, angry for being the one to come between a family. I can't go back into the clubhouse. I'm a mess.

'Peyton?' Amalia is pulling up in the car space near me. 'Are you okay?'

'I'm fine,' I lie, looking back towards Rob, who's still standing near his car, now on the phone.

'You weren't over there with Rob again, were you?'

'Not really. Why?'

'Look,' Amalia says, worry lines framing her eyes. 'Rob is Marnie's husband. I saw a photo of him when I was at her place last week.'

The tears turn to sobs, and I look away from Amalia, totally humiliated.

'Get in,' she leans over and pushes open the passenger door.

Climbing in, I search through my handbag for an old tissue or something to wipe my face. 'I just found out. I swear, I didn't know he was married.'

'Of course you didn't.' Amalia rubs my back. 'He played you, and he's lying to Marnie. He's a pig, and we have to do something about it.' Her tone changes, and she sounds frightening.

'What? Like tell Marnie? I can't do it. It'll break her.'

Amalia grips the steering wheel tightly and exhales loudly. Then she raises her voice, 'Men! They're such jerks.'

I dig a tissue out of my bag and dab at my tears, mascara coming off on the tissue.

'Look, I'll take you home. And then we can talk about what you want to do about this later.'

I nod. 'Thanks.'

I'm grateful that everyone is already down for an early night when I get home. Lucas is in his bassinet next to my bed, the monitor set up watching him and the screen probably next to Mum in bed. I switch off the camera and give Lucas a kiss. He stirs slightly but stays asleep. I curl up in a ball in bed and sob. How could I be so stupid?

Chapter 31

Marnie

Jasper lets out a sigh from his bassinet, and I can hear his legs kicking. It won't be long before that sigh turns to a high-pitched howl in demand for breakfast. I tap my phone screen, five-thirty. Not bad. We're getting so close to waking at a reasonable hour.

I roll over and am instantly reminded of yesterday. The pain in my leg has mostly subsided, but when I roll over it still hurts. An enormous bruise had come up last night, and I sweated through long pyjama pants all night to keep it hidden. Rob's asleep next to me, breathing heavily and oblivious to Jasper's little noises. I love and hate the maternal instinct that makes me jolt awake at any sound. I often envy Rob's ability to subconsciously block it out. I know I need to tell him what happened with Aaron, but he'll be furious with me.

I lift Jasper out of his bed and onto my chest. He looks at me with wide, hungry eyes before bobbing his head against me to find his meal.

Jasper drinks, and I scroll. Something to keep me from falling back asleep with him on top of me. The number of times I've gone back to sleep after a feed and woken in a panic because I don't remember putting Jasper down is too many to count.

There's a message from Amalia.

Hey, I need to see you today. Coffee this morning?

She's up early.

`Sure. Saint Cafe at 10?`

Her response comes back almost instantly.

`See you then.`

Jasper fusses, his little body wriggling, so I sit him up for a burp. Rob rolls over to face us.

'You were home early last night,' I say. I'd heard him come in about eight o'clock, much earlier than usual for a Thursday. I was already in bed.

'Oh, thought you were asleep.'

'Almost.' I smile down at him as I position Jasper on the other side to feed. 'Was the club no good last night?'

He lifts his head. 'It was fine, why?' he snaps.

I flinch at the tone of his voice. 'Because you were home so early.'

'Wasn't in the mood.' He rolls away from me.

'I thought you liked the guys down there.' I desperately want him to meet people and make friends. Maybe that'd fill the void that I know I don't fill for him.

'I do!' Rob raises his voice as he turns back to meet my eyes. 'Geez Marns, what's with the lecture? I didn't feel like being out, so I came home. Thought you'd be happy.' He rolls away again and mutters under his breath, loud enough for me to hear. 'Nothing I do makes you happy.'

Rob doesn't say another word as I finish feeding Jasper. I'm shaken. My chest feels tight. There's a lump in my throat, and I blink back the tears that prick at my eyes. Rob never raises his voice. We rarely argue. My thoughts drift to Fleur. I wonder if this is how she feels all the time.

I place Jasper back in his bed and take a shower. I let the tears fall freely, hoping the shower masks my crying as effectively as it blocks out Jasper's crying. He's fast asleep when I get out of the shower. I take the opportunity to get ready for the day. When he's asleep, my mind races through a thousand jobs I want to get through. Get dressed, brush my hair, eat breakfast, make coffee, and so on. I usually get through one before he senses my tiny achievement and decides to wake up. Today is no different. Oh well, at least I'll be dressed for Amalia.

I call out to Rob to say I'm leaving. It's the first time we've spoken since he snapped at me.

'I'm on late shifts for the next week, so I'll sleep in the spare room. I don't want to wake Jasper.'

'Okay,' I reply, before closing the door behind us. It's not unusual for Rob to sleep in the spare room when he does late shifts, but for a whole week and especially now, when we aren't in a great place...the timing couldn't be worse.

***

I arrive at Saint Cafe and spot Amalia at a table in the corner, bopping a laughing Lila on her knee. I weave the pram through the maze of tables and chairs and park it next to her.

'Hey, you been waiting long?'

Amalia shakes her head. Her dark hair frames her face, and her brown eyes don't meet mine.

A waiter approaches the table. 'Can I get you ladies anything?'

'Large almond latte please,' I respond, emphasising the word large.

'Tea, thanks,' Amalia says.

The waiter writes our orders on his notepad before cooing at Jasper, who's sucking vigorously on his dummy. *Argh don't stimulate my child when he needs to sleep.*

The waiter leaves and my mind drifts to Amalia's visit to my place last week. 'I meant to ask you at the surf club yesterday why you ran off so quickly last week. Was everything okay?' I ask.

Amalia looks down at Lila. She's taking deep breaths and hesitates, looking back at me. 'Not really. That's what I wanted to talk to you about.'

My stomach drops. Anxiety sits heavily in my belly, making me feel sick. I shift in my seat.

'When I was at your place, I saw all the photos of you and Rob.' She lifts Lila for a burp and then continues without looking at me. 'I left suddenly because I'd seen him before and was a little shocked.'

My eyebrows pinch together. 'Seen him before? Who? Rob?'

'I have a few friends whose husbands play down at the local cricket club.'

My breath hitches. I don't know what I'm expecting. I tilt my head.

'I go down there most Thursday nights and for functions and stuff. Anyway, I've seen Rob down there quite a bit.'

I try to keep my voice steady. 'Yeah, he used to play in Melbourne. He joined the club, hoping to meet some locals.'

'Yeah, well, one of the locals he met is Peyton.'

I screw my face up, confused. 'Peyton?'

'You know, from mothers' group.'

'Yeah, I know *who* you mean. I don't know *what* you mean.'

'Marnie, I'm sorry. But I've seen Rob and Peyton hooking up more than once.'

My chest tightens. I take deep breaths, but I can't seem to get any air.

'I don't understand,' I say, barely a whisper. Although it makes perfect sense.

'Peyton had no idea he was married. She found out last night.'

Tears fall for the second time today, and I begin to hyperventilate. I fumble through the nappy bag, searching for my pills. I pop one quickly and wait for it to have its calming effect.

'Marnie, are you okay?' she asks, as I dab at my tears with a napkin.

Am I okay? What a stupid question! My husband is cheating on me. Of course I'm not okay. This is all my fault. If I'd given him what he wanted, what he needed, maybe he wouldn't have looked for it elsewhere. But I can't compete with Peyton. She's beautiful and young. She's everything I'm not.

'One latte and one tea,' the waiter says, far too upbeat for this moment, as he places two mugs down before us.

'Thank you,' Amalia says.

The drugs kick in, my breathing steadies and the tightness in my chest eases. My initial shock and sadness are quickly boiling over to anger. Amalia watches me, pity written all over her face. I glance down at Jasper, thankful he's sound asleep.

Shaking my head, I whisper, 'I'm going to kill that bastard.'

Amalia frowns and puts her hand over mine resting on the table. 'I wanted to do the same when I saw him with Peyton last night.'

'What? You saw them last night?'

'Yep. That's when Peyt saw a photo of Jasper on his phone and pieced it all together. She's devastated.'

I roll my eyes. I hardly feel sorry for her.

'Anyway, after she found out, she wanted to tell you but I thought it might be better coming from me.'

I nod. A million thoughts rushing through my head. Hitting me the hardest is the fact I picked up and moved my entire life here for him. I left my job, my friends, my family, a house I loved and would've happily raised Jasper in. Now what? I'm stuck in some small town with barely anyone I know, and my marriage is hanging by a thread. A thread I'm close to snapping without a second thought.

'Can I do anything?' Amalia asks.

'Get me a weapon?' I choke out a laugh. 'I don't know. No.' I push my fingers hard into my temples.

'Are you going to talk to Rob about it?'

I shiver, the mention of his name making my blood boil. 'He's on nights for a week from today. I probably won't see him. Good news for him. I'm not sure what I'd do.'

'Well, call me if you need anything. I mean it.'

'Thanks.'

We finish our drinks in silence. I make sure it's late enough that I won't run into Rob before heading home. When I get back, I place Jasper in the bouncer and storm around the house. I don't know what I'm looking for, but I search anyway. I pull apart his cricket bag. There's nothing unusual except a brightly coloured Hawaiian shirt that's covered in something that stinks. It looks like it's been in here for weeks. Not exactly anything suspicious except that Rob is usually good at putting his clothes in the wash. I rummage through his drawers, look in his jacket pockets. Nothing. Each time, I'm careful to put everything back perfectly as it was. Then I come across the donut mug in my wardrobe. The cute gift I'd got him yesterday and hadn't even had a chance to give him. I burst into tears all over again before throwing it at the bedroom wall. It cracks in two, and then I sob even louder because I know I have to clean it up. By the time I finish searching, I'm so angry that I'm shaking. How the hell could he do this to me? After everything we've been through. And with a bloody teenager. What would the other cops think of him? It's disgusting.

Jasper cries out. The poor kid is probably sick of listening to the monotonous tunes that come out of the bouncer. Not to mention, starving. *I'm a terrible mother.*

After feeding Jasper, I take a long shower and cry...again.

Chapter 32

Peyton

I don't sleep at all Thursday night and spend all Friday morning crying. Mum ends up staying home from work to help me with Lucas because I'm a mess. I curl up on the couch under my doona on Friday afternoon. Lucas is asleep in his cot, and Mum sits in the chair opposite me.

'Peyton, what's happened? Talk to me. You're scaring me.'

I'm humiliated. I don't want to tell Mum what I've done. She'll be horrified. Even more so to know it happened at the cricket club, where our family is well respected. I've ruined everything.

I shake my head. 'I can't.'

'Of course you can. I'm your Mum.'

I sob loudly into my hands. Mum passes me a tissue.

Taking a deep breath, I stare down at my hands and pick at the soaking tissue. 'I've sort of been casually seeing a guy down at the cricket club. Nothing super serious. We chat and hook up occasionally.' Once on this very couch. But I don't tell her that part.

Mum nods. 'I figured as much. Didn't think it was Bree who suddenly got you so keen to go back there every week.'

My cheeks redden. Of course she knew. Mums always seems to know everything. Will I be like that with Lucas? Probably not. I suck at this gig. And I'm clearly hopeless at reading men.

'Well, turns out the guy is married. I had no idea.'

'Oh Peyt.' She moves next to me on the couch and puts an arm around me. It makes me cry harder.

'That's not all,' I manage to get out between sniffles. 'He's married to a mum in mothers' group.'

Mum's jaw drops. 'Oh.'

'Mum, I swear I didn't know. Like I knew he looked older, but I didn't know he had a wife and baby. Of course, I'd never have done anything if I knew.'

'Of course not.' She squeezes me tighter. 'You've done nothing wrong, sweetie.' She rubs my back as my sobs slowly subside, and I eventually fall asleep.

I wake up to two text messages on my phone.

Babe, we need to talk.

It's Rob. I delete the message. Then I go into my contacts and block and delete his number, too. I want nothing to do with him. He used me and lied to me. He's dead to me. Yet, I've still been wiping away tears since the moment I woke up. Rob's a jerk but I liked him. He's the first guy I've been with since Lucas' dad. I thought I'd never touch another man again after him. But Rob was hot and sweet and mature...and a liar, a cheat and a scumbag. I sure know how to pick them.

Looking back at my phone, the second message scares me a little.

Hey Peyton, it's Marnie. Can we meet up tomorrow morning? I'm going to take Jasper for a walk in the park at 9.

Amalia must've spoken to her. I'm so grateful that she was there with me last night. I told Mum I wouldn't make any friends at mothers' group. But she's sort of cool for her age, I guess. She's been supportive. I reply to Marnie.

See you then.

***

Lucas sleeps in his pram on the way to the park. He slept like an absolute champ yesterday and last night as well. It's as if he knows his mummy is struggling right now.

I drank a bottle of wine with Mum after I replied to Marnie last night. We watched a silly comedy and stayed up chatting. I finally got some sleep after labelling Rob every obscene name under the sun.

I spot Marnie on a bench near the far entrance to the parklands. I've been nervous all morning about seeing her, but I need to apologise even if I did have no idea what Rob was doing.

'Hey,' I say hesitantly as I pull up behind her.

She turns to me. 'Hey.' Her voice is soft and sad. Her hair is tied in a knotted mess and the dark shadows under her eyes make it look as though she hasn't slept in weeks. She's in the same activewear she wore to mothers' group on Thursday. I only remember because I own the same maternity leggings. The leggings along with her black t-shirt have milky spew stains all over them.

There's a long, awkward silence. I don't know what to do or say. I'm so angry at Rob for putting me in this position.

'I caught up with Amalia yesterday,' she finally says. 'She told me everything.'

Tears prickle at my eyes. 'Marnie, I'm so sorry. You have to believe me. I had no idea that he was married.'

Marnie takes a step closer. I struggle to read her expression. I expect her to be sad or angry, but she looks concerned.

'Are you okay?' she asks.

My eyes narrow. 'What?'

'Are you okay?'

I look around as though she must be speaking to someone else, but it's just me. 'Yes,' I lie. Then the tears spill over. 'No.'

Marnie takes my hand. 'You have nothing to be sorry for.'

What the hell! Her husband cheats on her with me, and she's the one comforting me. Now I feel worse.

'He's a lying bastard,' she continues. 'He lied to me. He lied to you. He betrayed his son. He doesn't deserve either of us.'

'You're not angry with me?'

'I was. But I've thought about it all night. I guess I believe you didn't know. I'm angry that I wasn't at the cricket club to catch the pig. Then I could've really shown him how to knock something for six.'

I let out a small laugh. Slightly relieved but slightly terrified of this version of Marnie.

'Anyway, don't they say exercise can help when you're angry? Let's walk and talk,' she says.

Marnie and I do a lap of the park. We talk about the babies, our pregnancies, Marnie's life in Melbourne, but mainly we talk about Rob. I tell her everything that happened and by the time I'm done, whatever the exercise did to relieve her anger, the conversation made up for tenfold. We're both furious. I didn't think I could feel any worse but learning about her struggle to fall pregnant and about Rob's job moving them out here away from all her friends and family, I'm even more angry that Rob has done this to her now. She deserves better. He deserves to suffer.

Chapter 33

Amalia

Are there any decent men in this world? I sit on the grassy hill that overlooks the cricket field and ponder that question. It's a beautiful spot. Lila is lying on a little blanket, gnawing away on a teething ring. Kya and some of the other partners are sitting on the hill too. They exchange small talk and picnic snacks.

I rarely come to the club for matches, preferring the events, but I needed to get out of the house. I never have Lila here with me, but I felt bad leaving her with Mrs Casci again. Hoping to avoid a visit from Marcus, I brought her along. But it comes at a cost. I'm stuck watching Rob, the do-gooder cheating cop. He's got his cricket bat in his hand, hitting the ball all over the park while the spectators cheer him on adoringly. Sickening.

'Heads!' someone nearby shouts, and I lean over the top of Lila to shield her body. A cricket ball lands a few metres away and there's more cheering.

'Great six, Jonesy,' Kya calls. Typical Kya, trying to be the cool wife, using nicknames and 'getting' cricket. She turns to me, 'How good is Jonesy?'

'Who?' I say, playing dumb. I can infer that Rob must be Rob Jones based on the fact it was him who hit the ball, but I will not join in and be his cheerleader.

'Rob. You know, the new guy.' Then she lowers her voice, 'You know, the one you say you weren't checking out the other day.'

I roll my eyes. 'I wasn't.'

'Well, he's bloody good. And hot! Are you sure he's married?' She winks at me.

It takes all my effort to hide my disgust. I've never understood the attraction to jocks. Why would I want to share my man with a ball or a bat or, in this case, both? Plus, this particular jock is a cheating bastard with a tiny baby at home.

'Pretty certain.' I nod.

'Damn!' she says with a twang.

She turns away, and I roll my eyes. Even if I told her the truth about Rob, I'm sure she'd only believe whatever her husband told her. The pack mentality of sport teams is another thing that puts me off jocks. Rob could commit murder, and his team would probably back him. I wish I had my own pack. Kya certainly isn't it. My mothers' group—I'm not sure. I'm working on it. Such a bunch of random, different women. But I suppose Marnie has already proven to be a decent person, and Peyton didn't know what she was doing. Fleur's full on, always a little frantic but trying to seem together. I suppose they're the closest people I have to friends for now. The closest thing I have to my Michelle.

My phone buzzes. It's Marnie.

Caught up with Peyt. She's a sweetie, hey? Thanks for everything.

I was not expecting that. I knew Marnie was going to reach out to her, but I didn't expect her to be so forgiving or get to the level of calling her a sweetie. Maybe she's in denial or it hasn't all sunk in yet.

You're a good person, Marnie.

I tap back my response, and she replies quickly.

How are you? Any more visits from Marcus?

No, but I'm waiting for it.

Come over tonight. Rob's working straight after cricket. Bring Lila.

That's tempting. I could rush home, grab the portacot and some clothes and hide out at Marnie's.

Be there about 6. Thanks Marns.

***

I get to Marnie's a little after six with a bottle of wine and a lasagne from my freezer. I may have lost my mum young, but she taught me never to go to someone's house empty-handed.

'Oh, you shouldn't have,' Marnie says when she lets me in, 'but that's perfect because I was going to order all of us a pizza.'

'All of us?' I ask, my brows furrowing. I don't want to share a meal with Rob.

'Yeah, didn't you see the group text?'

I'd been so frantically packing for the evening, I hadn't checked my phone.

'I asked all the mums but only Fleur and Peyton can make it. I hope you don't mind.'

I breathe out in relief. 'Of course not.' In fact, I'm excited. Now there are no secrets, I can relax. It'll be nice.

Peyton arrives first. I thought it'd be awkward, but it's as if she and Marnie are united in their hate for Rob, something that bonds them. She's left Lucas with her parents, and I can't help but feel envious of the relationship they must have with their grandson. My mum would've been an amazing grandmother.

Fleur arrives a little later, flustered as always, but still looking incredible in a jade-coloured dress. 'Sorry I'm late, ladies. Wanted to help hubby get Mia to bed first.'

Marnie shoots her a look. 'Are you sure it's okay to leave her?'

'Of course.' She smiles, but I swear there's a flash of warning in her eyes.

Marnie and I feed the kids early so we can stop counting every millilitre of alcohol we pour. Jasper and Lila settle quickly. They must know their mums need this girls' night.

We spend the next few hours eating lasagne and drinking wine at Marnie's dining room table. She has a beautiful house. The open-plan, modern kitchen has all the best appliances and a beautiful, tiled splashback like you'd see on *The Block*. It continues into a spacious dining room with an oak eight-seater dining table. Next to that is a large living room with one of those L-shape couches facing a big television mounted on the wall. That's where I saw Rob's photo the first time I came here. I think this entire living space is bigger than my whole townhouse.

During dinner, Fleur checks her phone constantly, never fully relaxing or engaging in conversation until we eventually tell her about Rob's cheating.

'I can't believe it. Marnie, I'm so sorry,' Fleur says, and she pulls Marnie in for a hug.

Peyton's usual confident posture slumps while we speak, and her face reddens.

'So, what are you going to do?' Fleur continues, not letting go of Marnie's hand.

Marnie shrugs. 'He's working nights for a while, so I can avoid him for a bit. Then, I guess, I'll talk to him. I want to kick him out, but then I also want to pretend it never happened.'

Surely, she isn't going to pretend all is well and move on. I can't let that happen.

Fleur nods but her gaze is miles away, as though she's been reminded of something else.

'I think you should confront him straight away,' I say.

Everyone looks at me and my cheeks warm.

'Really?' Marnie asks. 'Why?'

'Well,' I say, 'I was cheated on too. These bastards get away with it because they think we're weak. Don't let him go another day thinking he's gotten away with it.'

Marnie nods. 'You're right.'

'Seriously, do any good guys exist?' Peyton asks, sipping her wine.

'I was wondering the exact same thing earlier today,' I say.

Marnie laughs. 'You two are still young. You'll both find someone else.' But her laughter quickly softens and she blinks away tears.

The split in Marnie's maxi skirt slips open as she moves uncomfortably in her seat, revealing an enormous purple bruise on her thigh, bigger than my fist.

'Oh my gosh, Marnie. What the hell happened?' I ask.

The others immediately turn to Marnie and notice before she's able to adjust her skirt.

Her face reddens. 'It's nothing. I hit it on the corner of the kitchen table. It looks way worse than it is.'

Fleur's eyes narrow at Marnie. Does she not believe her as well? It doesn't look like nothing to me.

Peyton changes the subject back to men, although I'm not convinced that bruise isn't related to a man somehow. 'What's your secret, Fleur?' she asks.

Fleur flushes. 'I wish I could tell you. I'm not sure.'

Marnie clears her throat and for the first time tonight, there's a long awkward silence.

'Anyway,' I say, breaking the quiet. 'I don't think there are many decent guys out there. And the jerks, like Rob, deserve what's coming for them.'

Clinking our glasses together, we sing cheers to my statement. We don't need men in our life. We have each other. I think of my mum. One of my favourite memories was a trip we took to Queensland. Michelle and Lily were with us, of course. I reckon Lily and I were about ten. We went to a theme park, one with lots of rollercoasters and parades and junk food. A ten-year-old's dream. Mum and Michelle approached the ticket box and asked for a family pass. The sign said two adults, two children, so why not?

'Are you married or de facto?' the man in the ticket booth asked.

'No,' Mum replied.

'Then we can't give you a family pass.'

Now I know this is twenty years ago, but seriously, how backwards were some people? But my mum didn't take shit from anyone.

'For your information, these two girls lost their fathers at a young age so unfortunately, they don't have a 'family' as per your definition.' Mum used her fingers to make air quotes when she said family, and I honestly struggled to keep a straight face. 'Us four do everything together, like a family. So I'll ask you again. Can we have a family pass, please?'

The guy said nothing. Just took Mum's cash and handed us our tickets. We walked off laughing. That sort of thing happened more often than you'd think. They were my dysfunctional family. A family that Mum and Michelle created, and now I was going to create my own. Would she approve of the women I'd met? Could there be more than one Michelle in my life?

Chapter 34

Marnie

Rob sneaks into the house after his night shift, although if it's for my benefit, there's no point. I haven't slept at all. Of course, the first time Jasper doesn't wake for a feed overnight is the night that I can't sleep. When the other mums left last night, I tidied the house. I didn't want to have to do it today. The day is going to be hard enough.

The shower in the second bathroom fires up and the noise makes Jasper stir. I could probably settle him back to sleep but I want to get the morning feed out of the way so I can have this conversation. Amalia was right, I can't let him go another day thinking he's gotten away with it.

I place Jasper back in his bassinet and hope that he might have another hour of sleep left in him. I don't want him around to hear what happens, even if he doesn't understand. What if it leaves some sort of mental scar on his brain and then he starts killing animals and lighting fires as a teenager? No. He needs to stay in here.

In the kitchen, I put the kettle on and start making coffee. Rob comes out to the kitchen.

'Hey,' he says.

'Morning,' I say without looking at him.

'Alright, I'm going to bed. Long night.'

I take a deep breath. 'Rob, can we talk?'

'Can we chat later? I've got to be up for work again in a few hours.'

'It's important.'

He frowns. 'Is everything okay?'

I hand him a mug of coffee and carry my own mug to the table. 'Sit.'

'You're scaring me. Is Jasper okay?'

'Jasper is fine,' I say, looking in the direction of our bedroom, 'but we're not.'

He squints his eyes, confused. He must seriously think he's gotten away with it. There isn't a hint of worry on his face.

'I had drinks with my mothers' group last night,' I say, my voice wavering. 'They came here.'

There it is. A flash of something in his eyes. 'Okay,' he says. 'What's that got to do with me?'

'Peyton's in my mothers' group. But I think you already know that.'

He rubs at the greying hairs on his temples. 'What does that mean?'

'Are you really going to make me spell it out to you?' My frustration is increasing.

Rob says nothing.

'I know you've been hooking up with Peyton.'

He shakes his head. 'I think you're mistaken Marnie. I just know her from the cricket club.'

'Peyton was here last night. She told me everything.'

'She's lying,' he says. 'She's young, and she tried, but I said no.'

'People have seen you together.' I can't believe he's trying to deny it. At least have the decency to admit it once you're caught. 'How could you do this to me? After everything we've been through and the struggles to have Jasper, and you just throw it away.' Tears slide down my cheeks.

There's a pause and then his expression changes. He looks angry. 'You can hardly blame me, Marnie.'

'What?'

'Ever since you got pregnant, you won't touch me. I can't remember the last time we had sex or even kissed.'

Is he seriously blaming me?

'I know you've had your issues, but Jasper is nearly three months old. He should be in his own room so that we can go back to normal.'

Normal? Nothing will ever be normal again. 'Are you saying that it's my fault?' I choke out between sobs.

'I'm saying it's both of our faults. I'd have never been tempted by another woman if you made me feel wanted or showed me any kind of affection.'

I shake my head in disbelief. 'Get out.'

'What?' he says.

'Leave.'

Rob leaves the kitchen table and I place my head in my hands. I can't believe this is happening. He spends a few minutes in the bedroom and comes out with a packed bag.

'I'll be back when night shifts end and we can talk more. I'll stay at the station.'

I say nothing.

Chapter 35

Peyton

'How was your night?' Mum asks.

I'd had a good time at Marnie's. At first, I was nervous to go into Rob's house. It was like revisiting the scene of a crime or something. But it was totally fine.

'It was fun.'

'And what about that mum you told me about. The one whose husband...'

I cut her off. I don't want to hear her say it. 'Yeah fine. She's not upset with me.'

'And she shouldn't be.' Mum takes a loaf of bread from the pantry. 'Do you want some toast?'

'No thanks, I've had breakfast. Lucas got me up early.' Far too early. Thank goodness I'd cut myself off early last night and not had too many wines, otherwise this morning could've been painful. I wasn't keen to get drunk with the mums. Not when I wasn't certain where I stood with them all yet. Were they this forgiving? Were they going to turn on me? I needed to have my wits about me.

'Your dad and I are playing golf this afternoon and then staying at the club for dinner, so you'll be on your own. Will you be okay?'

Her tone irritates me. I'm not a child who needs babysitting.

'We'll be fine, Mum.'

***

Lucas falls asleep at seven, and I pour myself a glass of wine. I've got the house to myself and I can watch whatever I want without Dad commenting on how fake the Kardashians are, or how unrealistic it is that the Real Housewives would act like that in public.

Tonight's trashy TV option is *The Bachelor*. I'm about three episodes behind and avoiding the spoilers on social media has been harder than avoiding sand at the beach. This year's bachelor is a typical meathead with bright white teeth and a shiny forehead. He sighs dramatically as he contemplates who to hand his last rose to—the blonde girl in a sequinned dress who's swaying on the spot after too many drinks at the cocktail party or the brunette whose expression says, 'I collect your eyelashes and put them under my pillow'. The blonde gets the rose. Such a shame—the crazies make good television. I get up to refill my wine when there's a knock at the door. It's eight o'clock. Who could that be? Maybe Mum and Dad forgot their key.

I open the door and Rob is standing on the porch. Well, not quite standing. He's leaning on the bricks and he stinks of beer.

'What are you doing here?' I ask. My heart is racing. The last time I saw him, I'd found out about Marnie. I'd been falling for this guy, and in an instant it was over. Now he's here and part of me wants to punch him in his drunk, sweaty face and part of me wants to jump him right here on the doorstep.

'I had to see you.' He slurs his words.

'You shouldn't be here.' Why is he here? Marnie said he had night shifts all week.

'I don't know where to go. Marnie kicked me out.'

She did it. She confronted him. I thought she might've told us in the group chat, but I haven't heard anything.

'You deserve it,' I say. And a little voice in my head wants to add, *you can stay here.*

'I know.'

'Why aren't you at work?'

He shakes his head. 'I took a personal day.'

'And spent it drinking I'm guessing.'

'Mmm.' He looks at me closely now. As if before was just through his hazy, drunken lens. Now he sees me clearly. 'Peyton, I can't stop thinking about you.' He takes a step closer and tucks my hair behind my ear.

It tingles where his warm hand touches my skin.

'I'm leaving Marnie. I want to be with you.'

My mouth drops open. 'Are you serious?'

'Yes, I want you Peyton.' He steps closer again so that our faces are almost touching.

I want to lean into him, to feel his lips again. But Jasper's face pops into my head. Sweet, innocent little Jasper. And Marnie, who gave so much of herself to have a child.

'Go to hell, Rob.' I step back into the house and slam the door on him.

I pace the house, my hands clenched by my sides. I'm fuming.

My hands shake as I take out my phone and open the group message.

Hey. Sorry it's late. I know the kids are probably asleep, but I need some company.

How pathetic. I'm nineteen and hoping some middle-aged mums can come and hang out with me on a Sunday. For the second night in a row. What is happening to me?

Amalia: *Mrs C has Lila. I'll be over soon.*

Hanbi: *I'm working on some documents for tomorrow. Hope you're okay hun.*

Fleur: *On my way. Mia's asleep and Aaron's home.*

Marnie: *Jasper won't sleep. I'll be there in five, but I'll have to bring him.*

Peyton: *No worries.*

Zara says nothing.

I put some more wine in the fridge and raid the pantry for snacks.

'What's going on?' Mum says as her and Dad enter the kitchen.

Oops. Forgot about them.

'Oh, sorry. I invited the mums' group over. Is that okay?'

Mum's face lights up, and she bounces on the spot. 'Of course, of course.'

'I'll be in the shed,' Dad grunts.

'Out of the way, Peyt.' Mum shoos me away from the pantry. 'I'll make a platter for you all. Any allergies?'

I scrunch up my face. 'I don't know.'

She shakes her head as though I've committed a cardinal sin by not knowing the dietary requirements of these women I met four weeks ago.

'Go get changed,' she says. 'You look like a slob.'

I'm beginning to regret the invitation. Mum's about to turn into her crazy hostess alter ego who regularly appears when she's entertaining. So embarrassing.

I throw on some jeans and a t-shirt that doesn't have spew stains on it and go back into the kitchen. The dining table has been transformed into a grazing table of cheese, dips, crackers and fruit. Where did she find this stuff?

When the others arrive, my mum pours them all a wine and introduces herself. I give her a look that suggests she makes herself scarce. Apparently, she interprets it as *take a seat*, and she pours herself a wine and makes herself comfy at the table.

'Is everything okay?' Fleur asks.

I glance at Marnie who rocks Jasper in her arms. 'Not really. Rob came by earlier.'

'He what?' Marnie asks. Her tone wakes Jasper and he cries.

'Here, let me take him,' Mum says. She takes Jasper and, of course, with her magic touch, he stops crying.

'I'm so sorry, Marnie. He told me he was leaving you.' I look down at my hands. 'And he wants to be with me.'

'That asshole,' Amalia shouts.

Mum glares at her.

'Sorry,' she whispers. 'What did you say?'

'I slammed the door in his face, of course.'

Marnie half smiles.

'Did you speak to him, Marnie?' Fleur asks.

'Yeah. He told me it was my fault because I haven't been affectionate since being pregnant, and we haven't had sex since Jasper was born.'

Silence.

It's as though none of us knows how to respond.

Except my mum. 'Sounds like you're both better off without him.'

Cringe. This is humiliating. I don't need my mum rattling off cliched words of wisdom right now.

'Cheers to that,' Marnie says. She lifts her glass, and we all follow suit.

I'm shocked at how quickly we move on from that revelation. *Thanks Mum.*

Chapter 36

Fleur

It's been over a week since I told Marnie everything about Aaron and asked her to help me. But then whenever she calls or texts me about it, I ignore her. I'm pathetic. I went to her girls' night and then to Peyton's the next night as well because I knew a group setting would be safe, but anything Aaron related, I ignore. I'm too scared to leave him. For some reason, I've convinced myself that an alcoholic, abusive husband is better than no husband at all. That a gambling, deadbeat father is better than no father at all.

When she brought up domestic violence at mothers' group, I was furious. I'm humiliated enough that she knows what's going on. I don't want the whole town to know. Plus, the bruise on her leg wasn't from a table. I've had enough of those that look exactly the same to know that. But Rob, albeit a cheater, surely didn't do it. Who could it be? I push away the nagging thoughts that it could be Aaron because how could that happen? They've never met. But it's exactly the kind of move he likes. Knee to the upper leg, easy to cover up. I know from experience.

Aaron is at the track again, this time on a Wednesday. Yep, his gambling has now officially eaten into his work hours. Mia has gone down for a nap. I throw on some activewear and open the new exercise app I downloaded this morning. Aaron commented on my body last night, suggesting I haven't lost my baby weight as quickly as he'd expected. Maybe it'll make him happier if I lose a few kilos, and things will settle down.

I follow the exercises in the app, clenching my pelvic floor as it tells me to do jumping jacks. It doesn't take long before I'm sweating, struggling to catch my breath and dashing for the bathroom. I've gotten so unfit since finishing work and having Mia. Before I have a chance to finish and shower, Mia cries out.

'I guess that'll do,' I mutter to myself.

While I'm feeding Mia, Aaron stumbles into the house swearing. 'Damn Baz, setting me up,' he says, not noticing me on the couch.

'Hey hun,' I say, trying to hide my nerves. 'You're home early.'

His eyes pierce through me, ice-cold, furious. 'You taking the piss now, too?'

I shake my head. I've said the wrong thing.

'It's bad enough the guys at the track giving me rubbish tips, and now you think it's funny I'm home early because I've got nothing left?'

'I don't think it's funny. I'm just happy to have you home earlier,' I lie.

He cracks open a beer from the fridge and sits next to me. He tickles Mia's feet as she feeds. 'Hello, my angel.' His tone is sweet, completely different to the one he uses with me. Then, scrunching up his nose, he looks at me. 'What have you been doing? You're a mess. And you stink.'

My face flushes. 'Mia woke while I was mid-workout. Haven't had a chance to shower.'

Aaron scoffs. 'Is that your excuse?' He takes his beer outside, stopping at the door to say, 'Bring Mia out here when she's done. I can't sit near you.'

***

Mia spends most of the afternoon attached to me. It's been such a warm day, I assume that's why she's drinking more than usual. When she finally falls asleep at my breast, it's well past her usual bath and bedtime, so I put her straight to bed.

As I creep out and close the door behind me, Aaron grabs me from behind and slams me against the wall opposite Mia's room.

'What the hell do you think you're doing?' he yells in my face and places his hand around my neck.

A small scream escapes me, and he squeezes harder. I try to speak, but only a squeak comes out.

'I've told you before to stop coming between Mia and I.'

I'm struggling to breathe. My arms slam against his chest, but he doesn't move. He doesn't release his grip.

My vision blurs.

I'm going to die.

It's happening. I knew it would eventually.

And what about Mia? She's going to be left with him.

I close my eyes.

Mia cries out from the room behind me and he lets go. I drop to the ground, holding my neck and gasping for breath. She's a few months old and already saving my life. I need to do the same for her before it's too late.

Aaron goes into Mia's room. 'You didn't want to go to bed before having bath time with your daddy, did you?'

I lift myself off the floor, holding the wall for support. I walk gingerly into our bedroom, out of sight from where Aaron is now running a bath. Digging through my handbag, I find the folded-up card Rob gave us. I'd carefully hidden it in a tampon box. Aaron had snatched it and thrown it out, but I got it out of the rubbish bin after he passed out that night. I know I don't have much time. Aaron is singing softly to Mia, and her giggle rings out down the hall. My heart aches. She loves her daddy. But she doesn't know what he's like, not yet. And I never want her to find out.

I don't particularly want to talk to Rob after what he's done to Marnie and Peyton, but I feel like I have no choice. I quickly type out a text and send it to the number on the card. Then I delete the message so Aaron doesn't find out. I tiptoe down the hall, past the big mirror in the entranceway. My hand moves to my neck as I spy my reflection. The whole area is already a dark red colour. How am I meant to hide this one? It's summer. You don't wear scarves in summer. Tears sting at my eyes, but I'm determined to act normal, so he doesn't suspect me of contacting Rob. I take a supermarket made quiche out of the fridge and put it in the oven and set the table for the two of us.

The gurgle of the bath sounds and ten minutes later, Aaron joins me in the kitchen.

'She just needed her bath with me.' He smiles proudly. 'What's for dinner?'

So, we're doing this again—acting like nothing happened? Then he spies the dark marks around my neck.

'Oh Fleur, baby, I'm so sorry.' He pulls me into him and I flinch. 'It's okay, I won't hurt you.' He rubs my back.

I stand there frozen, swallowing back the bile that rises in my throat.

There's a knock at the door and my heart races.

'I'll get it, babe. You sit.'

The door opens, and I can't quite make out the conversation. The voices get louder.

'Fleur, come here!'

My breath hitches. What am I doing? What am I doing? I can't leave Aaron.

I throw on my dressing gown that's still on the couch from feeding Mia this morning and pull it high around my neck. It's thirty degrees outside. This looks ridiculous. But I head to the door, anyway.

Rob sees me, and his eyes narrow. I look down.

'Fleur, baby, tell this copper, once again, that everything is fine.'

I meet Rob's eyes. 'It's fine.' My voice croaks.

'Can I have a word with you privately, Fleur?'

Aaron doesn't give me a chance to answer. 'No, you may not. Unless you're arresting us or have a warrant, you can leave.'

I try to hide any sadness in my eyes, regretting my message to Rob, panicking about what my punishment may be.

'Fair enough.' Then he looks at me. 'Call if you need anything.'

Aaron slams the door before I can respond.

'What was he doing here?' I ask, trying to sound casual.

'I was going to ask you the same.' He steps closer to me. 'Says he got a report that there was a domestic disturbance at our address. Any idea who made that call?'

'No, of course not.'

'I better not find out you've been gossiping to those mums at mothers' group.' He moves closer again, and I step away, my back firmly against the wall behind me. Grabbing at my dressing gown, he feels around the pockets searching for my phone. When he finds it, he starts swiping and clicking, and I hold my breath even though I know he won't find anything. When he's satisfied there's nothing on my phone, he throws it at my feet, the screen cracking with Mia's face smiling up from behind it.

'I'm gonna kill that pig.' Aaron storms out the front door and gets in his car.

I can add drunk driver to his list of flaws. I fall asleep, gripping my phone under my pillow.

Chapter 37

Marnie

When I arrive at mothers' group, Fleur pulls up in the car space next to me. She gets out of the car wearing a turtleneck skivvy and skinny jeans. The cool change came through last night, but I wouldn't have called it skivvy weather. She has her big sunnies on as usual and smiles when she sees me.

'You okay?' I ask, immediately regretting it. I don't want her to think I'm getting involved again, even though the last thing she said to me was that she wants help.

'Can we talk after the session?' she asks.

'Of course. See you in there.'

Peyton walks up to the entrance of the community centre at the same time as me. 'Hey,' I say.

'Hi.' She smiles.

Sunday with the other mums brought Fleur, Amalia, Peyton and I closer together. Peyton's mum had waited on us while we laughed, cried, ate, drank. I told them about how much I'm struggling with my identity since having a baby and that some days I struggle to leave the house. For such a long time, I worried this made me a bad mother, but everyone has their own secrets and worries about being a mum. I left Peyton's house feeling like I'd finally made some real friends. The first real friends I've made since leaving Melbourne.

'Have you seen Rob again?' she asks.

It has been four days since I confronted Rob about Peyton. Besides a few texts to ask how Jasper is and some cold, blunt replies from me, we haven't spoken. It's not unusual for us to go this long without seeing each other properly. But we usually cross paths briefly when he gets home from night shift or before he starts again in the evening. He hasn't been home since I asked him to leave.

'I still haven't seen him. But he finished his last night shift this morning, so I expect he'll try to come home. Have you heard from him?'

'Not since Sunday. You doing okay?'

'Sometimes.' I shrug. 'Sometimes I'm furious. Other times I'm crying, mourning our relationship. And at times, I'm fine. Fine with the thought that it might be only Jasper and me, and we'll be okay.'

She smiles. 'He's lucky to have you as his mum. You're so strong.'

I return the smile, but I don't feel so confident about myself. Who knows if I'll continue to be strong? I'm so angry that he'd betray me like this, throw away our marriage and our new life with a baby to go and grope a teenager. But I don't know how to live without him. I barely cope as it is.

We head inside, Fleur coming in behind us. Zara and Hanbi are already there, sitting as far apart as possible. I don't think their friendship will blossom beyond today.

Liz looks around as we take our seats. There's one spot empty.

'Our final session ladies, I hope you've got something out of these discussions and possibly formed some friendships.'

The door opens and Amalia rushes in, looking frazzled. Lila cries out as she bumps the pram into the empty chair before sitting down.

'Sorry I'm late. I lost track of time.'

I smile at her. We've all been there before. Days disappear sometimes.

Liz doesn't even have a chance to continue before the door opens again. This time, two police officers walk in. It's the same two officers Rob and I ran into at the cafe.

'Sorry to interrupt,' one of them says. I can't remember his name. Today, his voice is serious and his face solemn, and I wonder if they're here to see Fleur about Aaron. Then, as if reading my thoughts, he adds, 'I'm Senior Constable Hartlett and this is Constable Mason. We're looking for Marnie Jones.'

My stomach drops, and everyone in the room looks at me.

'Can you step outside with us, please?' he says.

I look down at Jasper, who's sound asleep in his pram.

'I'll watch him,' Liz says, her smile laced with concern.

The room around me spins as I stand and follow the officers to the little foyer outside the main room of the community centre. We sit in the chairs that usually act as a waiting area for the Child Health Nurse.

'Mrs Jones, sorry to be seeing you again under these circumstances,' Senior Constable Hartlett says. 'We've been trying to get a hold of you for a few hours now, and this is certainly not the ideal place for us to talk.'

I don't move or speak. Why are they sorry? What's going on?

'Rob was found dead in Lakesfield Park this morning. We believe he was murdered.'

I shake my head, and my body goes cold. 'No, you must be mistaken. Rob worked last night.' I stand and walk back towards the door to rejoin the group even though I've always feared a visit like this and knew it was a possibility in Rob's line of work. But it can't be true.

Constable Mason takes my hand as I pass her. 'I'm so sorry.'

My legs give way under me and she helps me back to the chair. I no longer feel in control of my body. I'm floating, watching this all play out. A loud pained scream escapes me.

Chapter 38

Peyton

Liz stops talking when Marnie is taken out of the room with the police officers, and she moves Jasper's pram nearer to her chair. The silence is deafening. Seconds tick over, but it feels like an eternity. Through the window, Marnie sits, and I glance briefly at the other mums. I can't imagine what this is about. She is a perfect, do-gooder school teacher. Unless this is about Rob, but Marnie had said he was at work. Liz has clearly chosen to put the session on hold for a moment because we all sit there staring out the glass doors.

Marnie's scream sends shock waves through the room. Jasper immediately starts crying and Liz picks him up, worry shadowing her face as she looks out to where his mum is bent over in a chair. Amalia's face is like stone, unmoving, cold. Maybe she's unsure how to react. I'm on my feet straight away.

'No,' Marnie wails.

My stomach drops. My legs shake as I open the glass door. 'Marnie, what's going on?'

She looks up at me, her eyes filled with terror and tears spilling out. 'It's Rob. He's dead.'

I shake my head. 'No, no, no.' I keep repeating. Not Rob.

I fall to my knees. Zara takes Lucas from me, juggling Tiana in the other arm. Hanbi puts an arm around me and helps me back to my seat.

My sobbing is loud, and I struggle to breathe. Hanbi rubs my back, urging me to take deep breaths.

Liz looks down at Jasper, tears in her eyes. Staring down at a little boy who's completely unaware that he's lost his father. Zara is on her feet, baby in each arm bopping up and down to keep them calm. Hanbi continues to console me. Fleur is frantically searching for tissues. And Amalia—she sits there, silently, rubbing her wrist.

Chapter 39

Fleur

The male officer returns, leaving Marnie outside with Constable Mason.

'Unfortunately, Mrs Jones' husband was killed last night.'

Even though we knew, the confirmation sends a chill down my spine, and Peyton's cries become louder.

'Sergeant Jones' family are on their way from Melbourne now. They should be here in about an hour.'

Liz begins tucking Jasper into his pram and piling Marnie's overflowing nappy bag into the basket underneath.

'Unfortunately, we believe Sergeant Jones was murdered, and it's an open investigation. We have a few lines of inquiry, and some of you are amongst the last people to see or hear from him.'

My stomach flips and my cheeks heat. That's me. I saw him last night and he probably still has the message from me on his phone. Do they want to speak to me?

'Peyton Brookes and Fleur O'Connor?'

I raise my hand. 'I'm Fleur'. The eyes of everyone in the room burn into me. 'And that's Peyton'. I point at Peyton, her eyes red and puffy, and selfishly I hope she takes some of the heated gaze away from me.

'Please make your way down to the station. We have a few questions to ask.'

'Are we suspects?' I blurt out.

Hartlett's eyes narrow. 'We don't have any suspects at this stage.' He answers me. 'Is there a problem, Ms O'Connor?'

'No, of course not,' I reply, my voice wavering.

Chapter 40

Peyton

Mum picks me up from the community centre. There's no way I can drive. There's no way I can go to the police station with Lucas on my own.

I can't believe Rob's dead. Sure, I was furious at him, and heartbroken, but I didn't want this. And poor Marnie, poor Jasper. I stare out the front windscreen and the tears fall again.

'How does this even happen?' Mum says, her knuckles white from gripping the steering wheel. 'We don't have murders in this town. Do you know why they need to speak to you?'

'I don't know.'

I really don't. I know nothing about what happened to Rob.

'You said you haven't seen or spoken to him since his visit on Sunday. Is that true?'

'Yes, it's true.' I reply, annoyed. 'How the hell is a cop going to believe me if my own mum doesn't?'

'Sorry Peyt. It's just that the cops will consider your, uh, fling, a pretty good motive.'

Like that hasn't already occurred to me.

***

At the police station, people are manic. I suppose they have lost a colleague, their boss, and they have to investigate it, but it's a mess of tears, phones ringing non-stop, and crowds of reporters out the front.

'Ms Brookes,' Senior Constable Hartlett spots me across the room and comes over. 'Thank you for coming down.' He looks at my mum with Lucas in her arms and nods. 'You can wait here. Ms Brookes, follow me.'

Mum goes to protest, and I put my hand up. 'It's fine, Mum. I'll be back soon.'

Constable Mason is in the interview room when we walk in. She sits on one side of a grey table. There's a chair opposite her, and she puts out a hand indicating for me to take a seat. Hartlett sits beside her and fiddles with a machine on the side of the table.

Mason runs through some formalities, my name and age, and informs me that our conversation will be recorded. I know I've done nothing wrong, but my palms sweat anyway and my stomach churns, my breakfast threatening to reappear.

'Do you understand, Ms Brookes?' she says.

I nod.

'Sorry. I need you to speak for the record.'

'Yes,' I croak. I clear my throat and repeat myself. 'Yes, I understand.'

'How did you know Sergeant Rob Jones?' Mason asks.

My cheeks heat. I'm embarrassed to say I was involved with a married man, but I also feel suddenly protective of Rob. He's dead. He isn't here to defend himself, and I'm about to drag his name through the mud.

'I met Rob at the cricket club about a month ago.'

'And what was the nature of your relationship?'

'We had a few drinks together at the club, and we hooked up a few times.' I keep it PG.

'Hooked up?'

I try to mask my frustration and embarrassment. I know they know what I mean, but they want to make me spell it out for them. 'You know, kissed or whatever.'

'So, not a friend from Melbourne, then?' Senior Constable Hartlett raises his eyebrows and my back sweats. That was Rob's lie, not mine. 'When was the last time you saw Rob?'

'Sunday night. He told me he wanted to leave his wife for me. She's a friend of mine.'

'How did that make you feel?'

What is this? A police interview or a counselling session? I try to hide my annoyance, knowing it isn't a good look for my innocence. I take a deep breath. 'I was angry, obviously.'

The officers look at each other and scribble on their notepads. My chest tightens.

'Have you spoken to Rob since that night?' Hartlett asks, taking over the questioning.

'No. I blocked his number.'

'So, you were angry enough with him that you blocked his number?'

When I hear it, I realise how bad it sounds. 'Well yeah, he'd lied to me and I didn't want anything to do with him.'

'Where were you during the early hours of this morning?' he asks.

'At home in bed.'

'Can anyone confirm that?'

'Well yeah, my mum and dad were home, but they were asleep. And my son, Lucas, was with me.'

'Your son, I presume, is the baby out there who can't vouch for you?' Harlett's eyes are mocking.

I say nothing and Hartlett writes something else down.

'Ms Brookes, you have no one who can confirm where you were this morning, and you were angry enough at Sergeant Jones that you blocked his number. Was he bothering you so much that you decided to put an end to it?'

What the hell! Is this guy seriously accusing me of murder? I'm a bloody heartbroken nineteen-year-old with a little baby, not a psychopathic killer. My ears burn and my fists clench in my lap.

'Are you serious?' I slam my fist on the table. It stings. I know it's the wrong thing to do, but I'm so angry. How could they think this was me? Is a girl not allowed to be a little pissed off about unknowingly being the other woman in a marriage?

'One of our own has been murdered. I'm very serious right now.' Hartlett's eyes look a shade darker.

'Yes, I was angry that Rob used me, but he's not the first, and I'm sure he won't be the last. I don't go around killing every guy who pisses me off.'

Mum will be so disappointed in me for losing my cool. She's out there with Lucas while I'm in here doing myself absolutely no favours.

'Thank you, Ms Brookes. We're finished. For now.'

Mum and Lucas are waiting for me when I leave the interview room, but I'm not allowed to go home yet. On the way out, I pass Fleur. I hope she doesn't have to go through that as well. I offer her a half-smile, but her eyes are wide and she looks terrified.

I turn to Mum, 'And you wanted me to make friends in this damn mothers' group.'

Chapter 41

Fleur

'Fleur O'Connor,' Constable Mason says. 'How did you know Sergeant Rob Jones?'

I'd driven to the station and sat in the carpark for a long time. I knew they were going to ask me how I knew Rob, and I wouldn't be able to lie. There'd be records of his visits to my house. But I still wasn't sure if I was ready to tell them everything, to leave Aaron. Marnie had always said she'd help me, but I couldn't very well lean on her for support now. Everything had changed.

'Rob is married...um sorry, was married to a mum from my mothers' group. I met him in the park about a month ago.'

'Is that the only time you've seen him?' she asks.

I know they know about the house calls. I've always been a good liar. I'm constantly spinning the truth to explain Aaron's behaviour or brush off my injuries as careless accidents. But I can't deny things that are on police record. A lump rises in my throat. I think about Mia. Young, innocent Mia, who's out in the waiting room with Peyton's mum. Do I want Mia to end up at the police station again? Next time it could be my body they find.

A loud sob escapes me. Then the floodgates open.

Mason offers me a tissue. 'Mrs O'Connor?'

I pull myself together, just enough to speak. Between sobs and sniffles, I answer her. 'Rob came to my house a few times to inquire about disturbances.'

'When was the last time you saw him?'

'Last night. I sent him a message. My husband,' I pause and hesitate, 'he's struggling at the moment, and he has been losing his patience a bit.'

Mason's face hardens. 'Mrs O'Connor, has your husband ever harmed you or your baby?'

'Oh, gosh no, he'd never hurt Mia. He loves his daughter more than anything.' And that's the truth. My heart aches thinking of the way he tickles her after her bath, giggles ringing down the hallway.

'And you?'

I think about the women who came into the hospital multiple times, too scared to say anything. I go over my conversations with Marnie about what's happened at home. We can't live like this.

I pull down the top of my turtle neck to reveal the bruising around my throat. 'Last night he did this. But when Rob arrived, I freaked out and sent him away.'

'And your husband,' Hartlett says, 'did he know you'd contacted Sergeant Jones?'

'No,' I said, thinking about the last conversation I had with Aaron. *I'm gonna kill that pig.*

My breath hitches and I cover my mouth with my hand.

'Something wrong?' Hartlett asks.

Surely it wasn't Aaron. He's a violent drunk, but he's not a murderer. Someone who sings so sweetly to their daughter couldn't then run off and kill a cop. Could they?

'Sorry, no. I just,' I breathe deeply. 'I've never told anyone about Aaron before.'

I'm not sure they buy it, but Mason smiles anyway. 'You've done the right thing. We'll help you with your husband, Mrs O'Connor.'

Chapter 42

Marnie

Liz doesn't let me drive home, insisting I let her drive my car and she'd get a friend to take her back to the centre. My hands are still shaking and my eyes are puffy, so I agree.

Rob's parents and my sister, Kate, arrive from Melbourne not long after I get home.

'Marnie, sweetheart,' Rob's mum, Carol, pulls me in for a hug. She looks how I feel. Exhausted and broken.

Liz passes Jasper to Kate. This is the first time he's met his auntie. What horrible circumstances.

'The officers who called us said you'd have to go down to the station,' Rob's dad says. A retired officer himself, his voice and expression are void of emotion. 'I can take you down there if you like.'

'Thanks, Tom.'

'Why do they want to speak to you?' Kate asks, looking down at her nephew.

'It'll be routine,' Tom answers on my behalf. 'Don't worry, Marns.'

I nod but I'm not sure how routine it'll be. They've asked Peyton down there, so I assume the cheating is going to be discussed and possibly made public. Rob's poor parents lose their son and have to find out that he'd been doing the wrong thing as well. They have always thought he was perfect. We all did. Maybe they won't find out.

'Kate, there's some milk in the freezer. Jasper will need a feed soon.'

'Don't you worry about Jasper,' Carol says. She's barely let go of me since arriving, now stroking my arm. 'Kate and I will take care of everything here.' Rob's family has always been so supportive of us. His mum even drove me to some of our fertility appointments when Rob was held up at work.

The car ride to the police station is silent. Not in an awkward way, but in a way that makes my heart ache. Tom was always so proud that Rob followed in his footsteps.

Hartlett and Mason meet us when we enter. Tom takes a seat in the reception area and they lead me to an interview room.

'Mrs Jones, we're sorry for your loss. Rob was a great man and a respected sergeant here at the station.'

I nod. They run through some basic questions about who I am and then get straight to the point.

'Did you know your husband was cheating on you?' Hartlett asks.

I'm shocked that it's the first thing they ask me, and so casually, so coldly.

'Yes, I found out last Friday.'

'And had you spoken to Rob about it?'

'Yes. I confronted him Sunday morning.'

'You'd known for a few days and said nothing?' Hartlett presses.

'I hadn't seen him because of work and cricket. Didn't have a chance.' My voice is strong, despite the way I feel.

'So you found out that your husband was cheating on you and you let that simmer for a few days?' He looks at me, waiting for me to crack. To show any signs of weakness. 'When you confronted Rob, what happened?'

Tears prick at my eyes when I recall the conversation. It's almost more heartbreaking than the cheating itself. 'He tried to deny it. Then he blamed me.'

'You must've been angry?'

My cheeks flush, anger rising. 'What are you trying to say?'

'Where were you early this morning, Mrs Jones?' Mason asks.

'At home asleep.' Do they seriously suspect me? Is it because I told Amalia I could kill him? Did someone overhear? Obviously, that was a heat of the moment comment. I could never hurt Rob.

'Can anyone confirm that?'

'Am I a suspect or something?' I ask, my voice shaky.

'Can anyone confirm that?' she repeats.

'Just Jasper. Rob was working. So no. But our Google Nest records so you'd be able to see me at home.'

Hartlett nods and makes a note. Then he picks up a plastic zip bag from a box next to him. He opens it up and places its contents in front of me. It's a large watch with a leather strap.

'This watch was found next to your husband's body.'

I recognise it straight away. My heart sinks.

'It was covered in mud and we had to wipe it clean, unfortunately wiping away any evidence with it. It has an engraving under the face here.' Hartlett turns the watch over so I can see it even though I already know what it says. *For my darling, A.* 'Do you know who it belongs to?'

My mind is racing. She wouldn't do this, would she? If she did, she did it for me. For us. Peyton and me. Do I want her to be punished? For Lila to end up with Marcus? Bile rises in my throat and I swallow it back, hoping I don't look as panicked as I feel. One thing I do know from the last few days, is that these women are the closest thing to family I have in Lakesfield. I take a deep, shaky breath.

'I've never seen it before.'

***

After speaking with the police, Rob's dad drives me back home. The front of my house has transformed. There are reporters out the front and bunches of flowers lining the front picket fence. There are more people out and about than usual, supposedly walking. However, it's obvious they're there to gawk. They move incredibly slow and stare at us as we weave our way through the people waving microphones in our faces. I keep my head down and hold my breath until I get in the front door.

'You okay, Marns?' Tom says, putting a comforting arm around my trembling body.

I burst into tears. What the hell has happened? Rob is dead. My husband of a decade, the father of my child, is gone.

And I know who did it.

Tom pulls me in for a hug and holds me as I let it all out. We stand in the front doorway like this for several minutes before Kate and Carol find us.

'We thought we heard you come in,' Carol says, wiping her hands on an apron, and that's when I notice the smell of baking. Rob's mum is an amazing cook. Bless her. 'Come here, darling.' I'm like a relay baton being passed from one family member to the next. She holds me and cries as well. 'Come to the kitchen and sit,' she says between sobs. 'I've made a pie.'

'She wouldn't sit and relax,' Kate says, shaking her head. My sister sounds exasperated.

'Cooking is my outlet,' Carol responds.

'Jasper went down for a nap about fifteen minutes ago. He's fed and happy. Please eat,' Kate says.

'Thanks,' I say, barely a whisper.

We go into the kitchen and Carol serves us all a slice of pie.

'So what's going on?' Kate asks.

I shrug. 'I'm not sure.'

Tom jumps in. 'It seems like Rob was hit on the head with a blunt object early this morning while he was running.' Tom had been speaking to one of the other officers when I came out of the interview room. 'They don't have any suspects at this stage, but they do have evidence.'

That's when I remember the watch. I wonder if they showed it to Peyton and Fleur as well. I'm not sure if they'd recognise it, even though it always looked so out of place on Amalia. I can't believe she'd do this. I need to speak to her and the others. Amalia and Lila have been through enough.

'Do you mind if I go and lie down?' I ask, picking up my plate. I've barely touched my food. There's no way I could stomach it right now.

'Leave that, dear,' Carol says. 'Go and rest.'

I pop my head into Jasper's room where he sleeps soundly. How did they do it? Seems like everyone except me can get him to sleep in his own room. Then I hurry to my room. The room I share, rather shared, with Rob. Taking out my phone, I create a new WhatsApp group and start typing out a text to Fleur, Peyton and Amalia. But I stop. Senior Constable Hartlett warned me before I left not to discuss any details with anyone. This conversation can't happen on the phone. I delete what I've typed and start again.

Hey girls. Drinks at mine at 6.

It doesn't take long to get a response.

Peyton: Are you serious?
Fleur: You sure you're up for seeing people?
Amalia: I'll be there.
Marnie: Yeah, I need the company.

Fleur: *See you at 6*

Peyton: *Mum's made you a casserole. I'll bring it for dinner.*

When I return to the kitchen an hour later, Carol is still pottering around. Tom is outside on the phone, and Kate has Jasper on the lounge.

'He's hungry if you're up to feeding him?' she says.

Sitting down next to her, I take Jasper from her. It's a welcome relief given it's been hours since I last fed him, and I haven't had the time or care to pump. Yesterday, that fact would have freaked me out. I'd be anxious about my supply or the possibility of mastitis. Now, I couldn't care less.

'You okay, Marns? I mean, of course you're not okay. But like, how are you doing?' Kate stumbles over her words. I don't blame her. What do you say to someone whose husband was just murdered?

'I think I'm in shock. I don't know what I feel.' Stroking the thin wisps of hair on Jasper's head, I wonder if he has any idea what's going on. 'To be honest, I just want to be alone for a bit. Sorry.'

'Oh, don't apologise. We thought that might be the case. Tom and Carol are staying at the motel in town. I'm going to drive back to Melbourne and get Mum and Dad from the airport. They've flown back early from their trip.'

I go to protest.

'No, stop. Of course they're going to cut it short to be with you and Jasper. We'll all book the motel too, but if you want us at the house, we'll be here in a heartbeat.'

I rest my head on my little sister's shoulder. I haven't seen her in almost a year. She didn't make it to Christmas when the rest of the family met Jasper. She was overseas. Kate's only eighteen months younger than me, and we've always been close. Usually I'm the one comforting her after a nasty breakup or helping her decide what to reply to a Tinder match. I've been with Rob for so long that I would often live vicariously through her.

'Thanks Katie.'

Chapter 43

Fleur

I pace the hallway. Mia is asleep and Aaron still hasn't come home after he stormed off last night. Or perhaps he did, but noticed the police car out the front and then fled again. After my interview at the station, Constable Mason organised a police car and two officers to stay out the front of my house to arrest Aaron if he returned home. Even though their presence makes me feel safer, I'm scared. What if he talks his way out of it? He knows exactly what to say. That's why he's always gotten away with it. Then he'll be back here, angrier than ever.

I was relieved when Marnie's text came through. Usually, I wouldn't jump at the opportunity to hang out with a freshly widowed mother. *How depressing!* But she's been there for me and I need to do the same. Plus, it gets me out of the house.

Entering the bathroom to get ready for the evening, my reflection in the mirror shows dark red bruising around my neck. I'm done with hiding it. I wore a skivvy today. Ridiculous. It's the middle of bloody summer in Australia. I roasted during the police interview. There was sweat pooling at the bottom of my back from the nerves and the heat of being overdressed. Tonight, I'm not covering it up. It's time to be honest with myself and everyone else. I put some makeup on and run the straightener through my hair. I throw on a pair of jeans and a strappy top that also shows the bruises on my upper back. It's somewhat freeing to not cover it all up.

When Mia wakes, I feed her and then pack her bag for the evening. Marnie said I could use Jasper's cot for her to sleep in and that we're welcome to stay the night, but I haven't decided yet. I half expect the cops to interrupt my evening with a call to say they've got Aaron.

We arrive at Marnie's a little after six. Her street is packed with cars so I park in the driveway. My arrival sparks a flurry of people exiting the parked cars. I put on a jacket I have laying in the backseat and do it up high around my neck. I'm not ready to go this public with my battle scars. They hold cameras and microphones and shout questions at me. *What's your name? What are you doing here? Did you know Sergeant Jones?* I hold Mia tight against my body and rush up to the front door. Marnie lets me inside and the same lines of questioning are yelled out again behind me. Amalia and Peyton arrive together and rush inside after me. We go into the kitchen.

'What the hell?' Peyton says. 'They're like vultures.' She hands Marnie a dish. 'Twenty minutes in the oven, Mum said.'

'So, how are you?' I ask Marnie. The question seems stupid because how could anyone be okay after what's happened, but I also feel weird not asking. She's having us all over for dinner and drinks. What do we talk about? Shouldn't she be doing this with other people who knew Rob? His family? Her own family?

She shrugs. 'I'm okay at the moment but there's something important I need to talk to you all about.'

Mia takes that as her cue to scream, probably because I'm still tense holding her against me. I place her down on the playmat with Jasper. The three of us look at Marnie with anticipation.

'We'll wait and then talk while the babies sleep.'

I hate that. Now it'll be all I think about. Well that, and the fact my husband is missing and the cops are waiting to arrest him. No biggie.

'Speaking of, where are Lucas and Lila?' Marnie asks.

Amalia smiles. 'Mrs Casci has Lila tonight, but I can't stay late.'

'Night off for me,' Peyton says. 'Mum said I can stay as long as you need me. She asked me to pass on her condolences.'

Marnie nods. 'Thanks.'

Peyton puts the casserole in the oven as we all take a seat in the lounge so Marnie and I can feed the babies. The sooner we feed them, the sooner we can have a drink. Marnie's words. And it sounds good to me. I take off my jacket and Amalia gasps.

'Fleur!' she says.

Marnie gives me a reassuring nod. She was the first person I told. Her expression is warm and motherly. I don't know how she does it given everything she's been through, but she gives me the strength to tell the truth.

Peyton comes in from the kitchen and her eyes widen when she sees my back and neck exposed.

'What happened?' Amalia asks.

Mia drinks away innocently in my arms. She's the reason I'm doing this. 'Aaron did this to me. He's been doing it for years now.'

As soon as the words leave my mouth, I feel lighter.

Peyton has her hand over her mouth, and Amalia is looking down at her hands that are fidgeting in her lap.

'The other week he burnt my hand with an iron. That's why it was bandaged. And last night he strangled me. The other bruises are daily shoves, kicks, punches.' I sigh audibly. I did it. It's out there. 'The police are out the front of my house now, waiting to pick him up.'

'I'm so glad you told them,' Marnie says.

'I'm scared he'll get away with it though. He'll come home, sweet talk his way out of it, and things will stay the same.'

'They won't,' Marnie says, with certainty.

'Where is he?' Peyton asks.

'I'm not sure,' I say. 'Rob came by last night because I sent him a message saying I was in trouble. But then I chickened out of telling him. Aaron was angry and went out when Rob left and hasn't been home since.'

Peyton's mouth drops. 'Do you think it could've been him?'

'I honestly don't know. I don't know anything about that man anymore.'

'It wasn't him,' Marnie cuts in.

Chapter 44

Marnie

Fleur and Peyton look at me with the same confused expression. Amalia's expression is different though. The colour drains from her face, and she gets up to leave.

'I just realised, I forgot to give Lila's spare dummy to Mrs Casci. I need to go, sorry.'

'Amalia, it's fine. Sit down,' I say to her.

I have to assume that the events of the last twenty-four hours haven't hit me yet. I feel numb. Right now, I have this overwhelming desire to fix things. It's always been a part of my anxious personality. I think it's also what made me a good teacher. I like to problem solve. If there's an issue, I make a plan. When someone needs help, I find a way to do so. Today I can help two women who I care about and their beautiful daughters.

'What's going on?' Peyton asks. 'Did the police tell you who did it?'

Jasper has fallen asleep while feeding and I don't want to go into it all with him here. Call me crazy—I know a tiny baby won't remember this conversation, especially given he's sleeping. But I don't want to incriminate him.

'No. Look, give me a sec. I need to put Jasper down. Fleur, the cot's ready for Mia when you need it.'

'I'll come now too,' she says.

Peyton lets out a frustrated groan.

When we return, Peyton is trying to talk to Amalia but she's sitting there frozen, staring at the shelf of photographs in my living room.

I pour us all a glass of wine and we make ourselves comfortable in the lounge. All of us except Amalia, who still sits on the edge of her seat, ready to bolt at any moment.

'The police didn't tell me who killed Rob.' I pick up the conversation where I left it. 'But they showed me some evidence they found next to Rob's body.'

Amalia rubs at her wrist and stops when she sees me looking at her.

'It was Amalia's watch,' I confirm.

Fleurs gasps and covers her mouth.

Peyton turns to Amalia and stands up. Her tall figure towers over the trembling Amalia. 'What the hell have you done?'

I take Peyton's hand and pull her away from Amalia, gesturing for her to sit next to me instead. 'It's okay,' I say to her.

She's shaking her head, and she's probably right. I'm not sure if it will be okay.

Amalia clears her throat. She has tears rolling down her cheeks. 'I'm so sorry, Marnie. I don't know what came over me. He was running in the park like he had no idea what he'd done to you and Jasper and Peyton.'

'You can't just kill someone because you're angry,' Peyton yells.

I give Peyton's hand a squeeze.

'I know but something in me snapped. Lila's dad cheated on me and he's still making my life hell. I thought I was helping.'

A flicker of doubt fills me. Am I doing the right thing? She's clearly got issues. Maybe I shouldn't be helping her. It feels strange to turn my back on a decade of marriage with Rob, but then, that's exactly what he did.

Amalia continues. 'You're both strong women, like my mum, and I wanted you to realise that you don't need men like Rob. You deserve better.'

Peyton laughs. A manic laugh, and I'm worried now that she's not going to agree to my plan. A plan that now I'm even a little hesitant about. Fleur hasn't said a word. Her face is grey. She looks as though she may vomit.

'I'm not going to defend Amalia,' I say. 'But I think there's a better solution to this than us dobbing her into the police.'

I'd be freeing Rob's killer to protect someone else. But is Amalia the lesser of two evils?

'You want us to lie?' Peyton asks.

'It'll be the mother of all lies. But yes.'

Chapter 45

Amalia

The moment Marnie says she knows who killed Rob, I panic. This is it. The cops are probably on their way. I mean, how stupid of me to come for a drink at the house of the man I killed.

But she tells me to stay; tells me it'll be fine.

'Why don't you explain what happened?' Marnie says.

I don't know where to start. But I realise this is possibly my only chance of getting away with this.

'After Sunday night, when Rob blamed Marnie for his own cheating and tried to convince Peyton to be with him, I was furious. He wasn't even acting sorry. He didn't care. I spent days thinking about it, stewing on it. I couldn't imagine what Marnie was going through. I'd been cheated on but at least I knew he regretted it.'

I look at Marnie, and she nods at me.

'Then, last night,' I continue, 'Marcus rocked up again and tried to push his way in.'

'So your ex cheats on you and gives you hell, and you take it out on Rob? Why not Marcus? Why involve us?' Peyton asks. Her tone is venomous.

'I'd love nothing more than to put an end to Marcus' harassment. But I'm broke. I need him.'

'Lila would be better off with him than you,' Peyton says.

'No,' Fleur says. 'No baby should be with an aggressive man.'

'But a murderous mum is okay?' Peyton asks.

'Let's hear her out,' Marnie says, trying to ease the rising tension.

'After he left, I dropped Lila at my neighbours for the night. Mrs Casci was more than happy to help when I begged her for a night off.

'Anyway, I didn't know what I was going to do exactly. But I knew that Rob was nearing the end of his string of night shifts and what if he tried to convince Marnie to let him come home? I couldn't allow Rob to try and charm his way back to Marnie, to beg for her forgiveness. You're both better off without him.'

'I think we could have made that decision ourselves,' Peyton says.

'I drove to the park before dawn and waited. I knew he ran there after his night shifts.'

'What? How do you know that?' Peyton snaps. 'Were you stalking him?'

I look at the ground for a moment. 'Not exactly. But Marnie is pretty open about his roster so I followed him and tracked his routine. I needed to know what else he was doing. What else he was hiding. Marnie is my friend and I needed to protect her and Jasper.'

Marnie half smiles at me but something in her eyes makes me doubt she's truly grateful.

'It was so dark. It'd been raining and the breeze was moving the branches and making creepy shadows on the pavement. I was scared. Kya had left one of the guys' cricket bats in my car last weekend, so I grabbed it for my own protection. And I swear it, that was the reason I grabbed it.'

The three women stare at me.

'Anyway, when I walked into mothers' group this morning, everyone was already seated. I didn't realise I was late and when I checked my watch, it wasn't there. It wasn't at the park when I went back later either. The entire area was taped off.'

Peyton shakes her head. 'What the hell is happening right now?'

'I tried to see you guys at the station. I don't know what I was hoping to achieve. They wouldn't let me in though. When I got home, I was a wreck. I murdered a police officer. I tried to convince myself it was for the best. That I was helping. But now I've screwed things up for Lila and me.'

'Yeah, you have,' Peyton says, standing up. 'We need to call the cops.'

'Just wait,' Marnie says.

'Peyton is right. We can't cover up a murder just to help Lila,' Fleur says.

'My plan won't only help Lila though,' Marnie says. 'Amalia's watch says, *For my darling, A,*' Marnie tells the group. 'Fleur, you're worried Aaron is going to get away with his violence, but maybe we can get rid of him for good.'

Fleur's eyes widen. 'How?'

'I can go back to the station and tell them I panicked when I saw the watch because I knew its owner was a violent man. I'll tell them it belongs to Aaron and that you gave it to him. A... Aaron. It works.'

'No. I'm not doing this,' Peyton says. 'I'm not lying to the cops.'

'I don't expect you to lie for me,' I add.

'Like I said, I'm not defending Amalia,' Marnie says, and I flinch. I wonder if she'll ever forgive me. 'But Lila needs her, and we need to get rid of a dangerous man before he seriously hurts or even kills Fleur or Mia.'

'I'm in,' Fleur says. I'm not surprised that she agrees easily. The poor woman is covered in bruises.

Peyton still shakes her head. Marnie lifts her maxi dress to show the bruise we all saw the other day. It's yellowing now but still looks nasty.

'Aaron gave me this when I confronted him,' she says. 'We can't let him get away with it.'

Peyton sits there, rubbing at her temples. She doesn't look at any of us. Minutes pass until she says, 'Fine.'

Chapter 46

Peyton

It's been nearly two weeks since Rob was killed. Aaron was charged with his murder and because Rob had been to Fleur and Aaron's place several times for domestic disturbances, the motive was obvious. Paired with the watch as physical evidence, it was a cut and dry case. Only Marnie, Fleur, Amalia and I know the truth.

His funeral is in Melbourne today. It's going to be a large, official event, funded and organised by Victoria Police.

I've only been to one funeral before. One of the old guys at the cricket club died a few years back and Dad made the family go. I didn't know him well, but I remember the service. The tears, the music, the photos, the grieving family. I don't know how I'm supposed to get through today. How do I keep it together? How do I support Marnie? Thankfully, Mum agrees to come with me, and Dad will look after Lucas. She always knows the right thing to say and do in these situations.

Last night, us mums were texting in our WhatsApp group. Not the first one that I created with Hanbi and Zara, but the new one that Marnie made the day Rob died.

Amalia: *I want to be there for you guys.*

Marnie: *I really don't think that'd be appropriate.*

Fleur: I'll look after Marnie and Peyt. Don't worry.

Marnie: Are you sure you want to come? People know it was Aaron.

Fleur: I'm sure.

Peyton: My mum's coming too. I definitely don't think you should be there, Amalia.

I had been cold with Amalia ever since that night at Marnie's. The night we all found out what happened. I know I didn't have to agree, but when I saw Fleur's bruises and then Marnie's leg, I didn't want to be the one to send Fleur and Mia home to that monster. But now I've covered up a crime and protected a woman I don't trust. And everyone's acting normal. Amalia thinks we're all best friends. That we're bonded together forever because of what happened. I think we should never speak to one another again. But then Amalia says things like *You're only nineteen* or *You don't understand.* She's really pissing me off.

Dressing in the most conservative black clothing I own, I wonder if the black skirt and shirt scream *other woman*, or if I will fit in with the rest of the mourners?

Luckily for me, everyone wants to protect the heroic police officer who died trying to help a victim of domestic abuse. No one wants to out him as a cheater. Marnie plays the grieving wife. I play a friend of Marnie and anyone who recognises me as otherwise keeps their mouth shut.

I stand with Fleur as she offers her sincerest apologies to Rob's family. I hold her hand tightly as they tell her that her apology is unnecessary. But they're unable to hide the pain and anger on their tired faces.

On the way home, Mum drives. She leans over and pats me on the leg. 'You did well today, sweetheart. That can't have been easy.'

I half smile at her.

'Where was Amalia today?' she asks.

I look out the window, hoping to hide any sign that I'm lying. 'Babysitter fell through.'

'Your dad would've taken Lila.'

'Mum, I've seen you text Dad six times today. He has his hands full.' I've been reminding myself all day that my dad had two kids once, and all he needed to do was keep Lucas alive. My baby might be covered in milky spew and watch war movies all day, but he'll survive.

'So what were you three whispering about at the wake? I thought I had something on my face the way you all looked at me and went silent when I came over.'

Is she onto us? Surely not. We never discuss what we did in our WhatsApp group. We're so careful. We agreed to never bring it up. When the news about Aaron broke, I was with Mum and played the shocked friend perfectly. Mum made Fleur a meal, and I delivered it to her like a friend, not an accomplice.

'I don't remember,' I lie. We'd been discussing how Fleur was coping. All the people at the funeral considered her husband a murderer. Even though she was glad to be rid of him, it was hurting her to hear it. 'Probably the cheating thing. We didn't want people knowing about that side of him.'

'Right,' she says, sounding unconvinced.

I feel terrible lying to her. It's my mum. The woman who has not left my side as I raise a baby on my own in my teens. The woman who would drop anything to help Lucas or me.

But I'm protecting a murderer. I helped put a man behind bars for a crime he didn't commit. She can never know.

Chapter 47

Marnie

My fridge and freezer look like a Tupperware catalogue. Containers of all different shapes and colours take up most of the space. They're filled with various meals, snacks and treats that keep being delivered through my revolving door of visitors. I'm grateful to not have to think about groceries or cooking but I'd love a day where I don't have to politely let someone in and work out how to best answer the standard question, *How are you feeling today?*

Because the truth is, I don't know how to feel. It's been a few days since Rob's funeral, and I thought I'd feel different after that, better maybe. Instead, my mind hops erratically from heartache to relief to anger. I'm not even sure who I'm angry with. Rob? Amalia? Myself?

Jasper sleeps in his cot, one silver lining to all of this. The circumstances have made him flexible when it comes to sleep. He'll sleep wherever, whenever now. I'm grateful that he has no idea what's going on. I'll make sure he never knows what his dad did. He'll grow up and learn about his father, the hero, who died protecting others.

In desperate need of a shower and fresh clothing, I grab a t-shirt and leggings from the wardrobe. A clunking sound comes from the shelf as I pull out the clothes. It's the mug I bought Rob, the one that broke. It's still in two pieces, cracked right down the middle of the donut with heart shaped sprinkles. How fitting.

I take the two pieces of broken mug into the kitchen and find the superglue. I don't know why I'm bothering to fix it. I want to feel in control of something. I want to make something right. I carefully line up the two parts and hold them together. When I let go with one hand and hold the handle, it stays together. I fill it with water and hold it in front of my face. Water dribbles out of one of the cracks. *Fail*. I tip out the water and throw the mug in the bin. Then I drop to my knees and sob.

I know I can call Kate or my parents and they'd drop everything to be here. But they've gone back to Melbourne now that the funeral is over. They didn't love staying at the motel, and I couldn't have handled them being here all the time. It's the strangest feeling, this grief. I want my mum here to wrap me up in her familiar hug and say all the right things to make me feel better, and at the same time, I just want to be alone.

I get up off the kitchen floor and splash water on my face. Jasper is still asleep, so I take a shower. When I get out, there are a bunch of unread messages in the *Lakesfield Summer Mums* WhatsApp group. *The original group.*

Fleur: *Hi mamas. Just reminding you all that our first unofficial mothers' group session is at my place tomorrow. Who's in?*

Ugh. Fleur had caught me on an *okay* day when she mentioned organising this. She'd dropped off a brownie slice. The look of it must have lifted my mood momentarily because I agreed it was a great idea. Now, I can't think of anything worse.

Hanbi: I'll no longer be able to take time off work on a Thursday for these catch ups. Sorry. Hopefully see you ladies around.

Hanbi left the group.

Amalia: Can't wait. Lil and I will be there.

Can't wait? Really? Her excitement angers me. I don't regret framing Aaron. Fleur and Mia are safe now. But each day, when I don't feel better, when I realise I've lost so much, my feelings toward Amalia shift. I chose to protect her. But I'm not sure I can keep hanging out with her and being *one of the mums* with her. That's weird, right? Spending time with your husband's murderer. Can't be healthy.

Peyton: See you tomorrow.

Zara left the group.

Well, that doesn't surprise me. Zara has been MIA since the cops showed up at mothers' group the day Rob died. I saw her in the park the day before the funeral and called out to her. She definitely saw me, her expression went from calm to alarmed in an instant. She pretended not to hear or see me and kept walking. My husband was murdered and that's how she treats me. She doesn't know what went down with us mums later that night, so really, she's just a bitch. No huge loss.

Marnie: I'll be there. Need me to bring anything?

Fleur: Absolutely not. And don't feel pressured to come if you aren't up for it tomorrow. By the way, looks like we could probably use our other group. Just us four again.

Just us four again. Dangerous.

***

When I arrive at Fleur's place, she greets me with a hug. I remember the first hug she gave me on the day we met. How was that only two months ago? So much has changed.

For Fleur, it's changed for the better. She looks great. Happy. Rested. How can a single mum to a baby look rested? But then what was going on before is much worse than standard parent exhaustion. Her new life probably *is* restful in comparison.

'How are you feeling today?' she asks me.

There it is. The question I get daily.

'I'm fine,' I lie. I don't tell her that I fished Rob's mug out of the bin and put it on his bedside table, or that I washed his cricket gear because the finals are coming up, or that I didn't sleep a wink worrying that Aaron would escape jail knowing what we did. 'Just a bit tired.'

Peyton and Amalia arrive not long after me. The babies lie on the playmat together. They're completely engrossed in their own activity, basically unaware of one another. Jasper is holding his dummy above his face, waving it around. Lucas is propped on his elbows, putting the other babies to shame with his tummy time. Mia and Lila kick at some toys hanging from the activity gym. This might be the first time since we met where they're all awake and not feeding. A few weeks ago, I'd have rushed to take a photo. These four babies who met so young and would grow up to be friends. Now, I'm not so sure. I don't want a photo. I don't want memories of Jasper playing with the babies of women who helped cover up the murder of his father. *Seriously, what am I doing here?*

Fleur brings in a bottle of wine and some glasses. The WhatsApp conversation had later turned into what these group sessions would involve, and it was a unanimous decision that wine must be included.

Fleur pours us all a glass, and I wait for someone to speak. Besides wine and deciding who would provide snacks, we never discussed what we'd do once we were together. We can't talk about Rob or Aaron. We agreed to never talk about that. But I know that's probably all anyone is thinking about. It's all I'm thinking about.

'Isn't it crazy that we've only known each other a few months,' Amalia says. She doesn't sound like the timid person we met a few months ago. 'And now look, we're all single.'

No one says anything for a moment.

'Kind of inappropriate, don't you think?' Peyton asks.

'Sorry,' she says. 'But we have each other now is what I mean. We'll have so much fun.'

I take a big sip of wine, hoping it hides my shock at what she's saying. She clearly isn't feeling the tension that I notice when we're together. This group is built on lies and secrets. Its expiry date looms.

'I was thinking about signing Lila up for baby sensory classes. They're on a Tuesday. Anyone keen?' Amalia asks.

'I'm not sure I can afford anything like that yet,' Fleur says. 'I'm working through all the Centrelink stuff to get myself some financial assistance, but it's so complicated.'

I glance at Peyton, hoping she'll say something because I don't know how to respond.

'Think I'll start working Tuesdays soon,' Peyton says.

I wait for Amalia to look to me for an answer but instead Peyton's response sends her off on another tangent.

'I'm starting work too,' Amalia says. 'Where are you sending Lucas for childcare? We should send the kids together.'

What the hell is wrong with her? It's as though nothing has happened. No. Actually, it's as though something has happened and changed her life for the better. I've never heard her speak so much or with such excitement. She killed a guy just weeks ago. This isn't normal.

Chapter 48

Fleur

When we lived in Melbourne, when Aaron was a different person—the person I fell in love with—I used to hate spending the night alone. The bed felt empty and cold, and every creak of the house or scratch of the trees outside sent me into a panic about a burglar or axe murderer. Now, spending the night alone in our house, I've never felt safer.

It's been almost three weeks since the police arrested Aaron. Thankfully, I wasn't home. I haven't seen him since the night he strangled me and stormed off. I've given many detailed reports to the police over the last few weeks, and they hope to add some assault charges to his murder charge.

I thought I would miss Aaron or that I'd find it challenging being a single parent. But now I realise I've been a single parent the whole time. Only now, I'm not fearing for my safety or my life. It's an amazing feeling to wake up in the morning and know that I'm not going to be punished for saying the wrong thing, cooking something the wrong way or wearing something that isn't appropriate.

However, I don't wake up feeling amazing today. Today is the day I visit Aaron at the remand centre. He wasn't granted bail, he couldn't afford it anyway, and so he'll be there until the case goes to trial. The other mums keep telling me I'm crazy for visiting him, that it's like returning to the scene of the crime. What if he works out what we did?

What if he tricks you into saying something? But I need to do this for me. Peyton and her mum are looking after Mia this morning. There was no way I'd take her with me.

It takes me a few hours to get to the remand centre and I consider turning back so many times. My palms are sweaty and I've chewed all my nails. Signs reading *Metropolitan Remand Centre* direct me toward a large grey building. It's ominous enough without even thinking about who's in there and what they might've done. I park the car and go into the building. During the last few days I learnt that visiting a prison is more complicated than entering a foreign country. I'm here well before my scheduled visit so I can register and be reminded of the many rules that apply when visiting a prisoner.

I'm led into the visitor centre and seated at a small table opposite an empty chair. Minutes drag like hours before a guard brings Aaron into the room. Long knotted hair hangs around his face and his usual stubble is now thick around his jawline. When he sees me, he smiles. It puts me off guard for a moment, but I remember that he doesn't know that I know the truth about Rob. And I'm guessing he doesn't yet know about the statement I gave the police.

He sits opposite me. 'Fleur, baby, I've been hoping you'd visit soon. I miss you so much. How's Mia?'

I'd expected rage. A version of Aaron that I am used to by now. I'd prepared myself for it and found strength in the fact that he couldn't hurt me in here. But smiling, loving Aaron? I wasn't prepared for this. Do I go along with it? Or do I say what I came here to say?

'Mia's fine,' I say, emotionless.

He puts his hand out to touch mine. 'Are you okay? I'm sorry I'm not there with you. I know how much you hate being home alone.'

'I'm fine.' I pull my hand away.

He tilts his head at me, looking into my eyes that I'm straining to keep from tearing up.

'What's going on?' he asks. His tone has changed. I'm sensing the transition from love to rage that I know too well.

'Nothing,' I say.

'Well, why are you here? I've been asking you to come for weeks.'

'I'm here to tell you that,' I pause. My heart aches remembering the boy I met in high school. Innocent, sweet, so much ahead of him. Ahead of us. 'Um, I'm leaving you. I won't be here when you get out. Nor will Mia.'

His chair screeches as he pushes it out, jumping to his feet. His hand slaps the table and other visitors turn to look at the commotion. My cheeks burn.

'Calm down, Mr O'Connor, or this visit will be cut short,' a nearby guard says.

Aaron sits back in his seat and clasps his hands together tightly. So tight that his knuckles whiten and I can't help but notice his wedding band. My heart aches.

'You can't do this, Fleur. I didn't kill anyone. I've been framed.'

'I don't believe you,' I lie.

'You have to believe me. Don't take my little girl away. You know how much she means to me.'

I do. And it hurts me to keep them apart, but she deserves better. I need to show her what a strong woman looks like. I say nothing, too scared I might cry if I do.

'Fleur, I didn't go near that cop. I was angry after he came to the house and I went out walking. I had some drinks on the beach on my own and fell asleep.'

I shake my head. 'You can't prove that.'

'But you know me. You know I could never kill someone.'

Suddenly, I don't feel like crying. Instead, I want to laugh. *Is he serious?* I've feared for my life on more than one occasion with Aaron. He absolutely could kill someone. Sure, he didn't kill Rob, but I could've been the next body found.

I hold up my hand where a faint scar from the iron burn remains. 'This is the only mark I have left to remind me that you definitely could kill someone. The last four weeks, my body has finally returned to normal after being a canvas for you to do your damage on. The bruises are gone, my neck and throat no longer hurt. And you'll stay here and pay for those crimes too.'

His jaw drops. He definitely didn't know about my statement.

'You'll be hearing more about that from the police.'

I stand and turn to walk away. He grabs my wrist and leans over the table, so his face is near mine. The guard is quick to move toward us but not before Aaron speaks.

'I did those things to make you better,' he says, voice low and venomous. 'You should be grateful.'

Then the guard grabs him by the arm and takes him out of the visitor centre. I drop back into the seat to compose myself.

Over the past few weeks I wondered if I'd done the right thing setting up Aaron. Was I robbing Mia of a father? Was I acting hastily? Perhaps I hadn't given him a chance to change. But now I know. I needed this meeting with Aaron. I needed it so I can feel at peace with what we've done.

Was it worth it? Yes. Do I owe the other mums? Yes.

I owe them my life.

Chapter 49

Peyton

Lakesfield Cricket Club is putting on a memorial match for Rob today. I'm glad Rob kept all our public hookups in the privacy of the carpark or on the dark abandoned clubhouse balcony, because the funeral and today would've been awkward if the other guys here knew about us.

I go to the match with Marnie, my parents and the babies. I intend to drink a lot. When I get to the bar, I expect Jake to make a joke about me flirting with a married man, but I suppose making jokes about a dead cop isn't appropriate and for that I'm grateful.

I take a round of drinks outside. Mum and Dad said they'll take Lucas and Jasper home later so that Marnie and I can enjoy ourselves. They're treating me like a wounded bird lately and have all but adopted Marnie and Jasper too. I'm not complaining though. I am wounded. My issue is I feel constantly guilty about their care for me. They don't know that they're actually caring for their daughter, the criminal. Their daughter who framed another person for murder. Their daughter who lied to the police.

When Mum checks on me every night and gives me a kiss like I'm a child again, I want to curl up in her arms and tell her everything.

When Dad takes Lucas out of my arms so that I can take a long shower or have some breakfast, I want to drop to my knees, cry and tell him the truth.

If they know I'm acting strangely, they don't say anything. It's probably part of the whole protect poor Peyton routine.

The match opens with a minute of silence and a presentation announcing that the Lakesfield Cricket Club best and fairest award will be renamed the Robert Jones medal. He hadn't played at the club long, but it seems he made quite an impact, as this is met with tears and applause. Marnie smiles at the announcement, nodding her head in gratitude.

The game starts and five or six drinks later, it's over and my parents are taking the babies home. Marnie and I head inside. She's greeted by some of the players who she met at the funeral. They give her hugs and promises to help with the lawn and things around the house. I sneak off to get more drinks.

When I return, she's standing with Amalia. Ugh. I'm not in the mood for her. I've done what I needed to do. I've agreed to keep the secret. Do I have to hang out with the secret? Do I have to buy the secret drinks?

'Hey Peyt,' she says, and her voice irritates me more than ever. 'Mrs Casci gave me the night off. Sounds like everyone here is in for a big night.'

'Well it's a memorial. They want to celebrate Rob's life,' I say. 'Taken too soon, as they say,' I add.

Amalia narrows her eyes. 'Indeed.'

Marnie's chin drops.

'Amalia,' I whisper, 'do you think it's appropriate that you're here?'

'We're in this together.'

I shake my head. 'No, we're in this because we want to help Fleur,' I say, hoping no one is looking. We're not supposed to discuss what happened, but my blood is boiling, and I can't stand the sight of Amalia right now.

'It's fine,' Marnie says softly, glancing around, presumably thinking the same thing as me.

'It's not fine. I agreed to help you, Amalia. I didn't agree to be best friends and go out drinking with you,' I pause and drop my voice down to the softest whisper, 'at an event to honour the man you murdered.'

Marnie takes my hand. 'We should go.'

Amalia follows us out. 'Wait,' she calls.

We begin walking through the carpark. We were always going to walk home but hadn't anticipated that it'd be this early.

'Wait a sec.' She runs to catch us.

We stop and turn to her. Marnie looks at the gravel of the car park below her feet. I raise an eyebrow at Amalia. 'What?' I ask.

'I'm sorry,' she says, 'I shouldn't have come tonight. That was silly. You girls are my best friends and I wanted to be here for you.'

I almost scoff. *Best friends*. I'd barely call her a friend at this point. She's the woman who didn't tell me Rob was married right away, then killed him, then agreed that we should cover it up and then wants to hang out with us. Is she bat-shit crazy?

'Amalia, we need to take things easy until everything dies down,' Marnie says, always pragmatic. 'Then we can hang out.' Also, a people pleaser.

Amalia nods, her lips turned down. 'I'll just see you at mothers' group then,' she says and walks away.

Even that's too much for my liking.

Chapter 50

Marnie

My phone pings in my pocket as I place a sleeping Jasper down in his cot. *Dammit.* I always forget to put it on silent before beginning the process of settling him to sleep. He doesn't stir. Dodged a bullet this time.

It's Peyton writing in the WhatsApp group.

Hey mamas. I'm not feeling well so won't make today's session. See you soon.

A moment later a text message comes through to me. It's Peyton.

Hey Marns. Sorry I can't be around her today. Hope you and Fleur have a good time with the babies. Walk later?

Her. Amalia. Peyton can't stand to be around Amalia. I can hardly blame her. I know she's struggling with the whole situation. Especially how normal Amalia is acting. It bothers me too, but we're bound to her for life. We're always going to have Rob's death tying us to one another. If one of us says something now, we all suffer. I figure *keep your enemies close* right? And even that isn't fair because she isn't my enemy. She thought she was helping me, us.

I shoot back a text agreeing to meet up later.

When Jasper wakes up, I drive us over to Amalia's place for our session. Fleur is already there. I put Jasper on the living room mat with Mia and Lila and join the other mums in the kitchen.

We exchange hellos and hugs. It's awkward, and I wonder if that feeling will ever go away.

'How was the prison visit?' I ask Fleur when we're seated with a glass of wine in the living room.

She shrugs. 'He didn't know I had given a statement about him to the police.'

'Does he know now?'

'He knows I won't be waiting for him when he gets out and any day now he'll be informed about my report.' She takes a big sip of her wine. 'You know, he tried to tell me the abuse was to help me be better.'

I shake my head. 'He's in the right place, the pig.'

Amalia smiles. 'You really did create the perfect plan, Marns.'

Her tone is sickly. It's as though she's sucking up to me, sweet-talking me. I don't want kudos for a plan that covers up my husband's murder. I want to forget it ever happened.

I ignore her.

'Anyway,' I say. 'What else is news?'

Fleur smiles. 'Well, I'm going back to work. I'm so excited.'

'That's great. When do you start?' I ask.

'I start in a month, but first, Mia and I are going to downsize. I found a little place to rent just out of town, closer to the hospital.' She holds up crossed fingers. 'Hopefully I can sell the house soon.'

I smile, even though my heart sinks. Fleur was the first mum I grew close to in this group. She's now one of my closest friends. We've been side by side during the most heart wrenching, painful events of our respective lives.

'You can't move,' Amalia says.

'Why?' Fleur and I say at the same time.

'We have a bond. We need each other. Our kids need each other.'

Fleur's brow furrows. Her face matches my confusion.

'I need to move. I can't afford my house and the childcare near the hospital is cheaper.'

'But our kids were going to go to childcare together. Here. In Lakesfield.' Amalia's voice is panicked.

'Sorry, I can't.'

'You don't need to apologise,' I say, shooting a warning at Amalia. 'This is exciting. Congratulations.'

Fleur smiles. 'Thanks.'

'Sorry. That's great Fleur,' Amalia says. 'We should all take a trip with the babies before you start work. We could get a big Airbnb somewhere with lots of space for the babies.'

I inhale sharply. Is she serious right now? I have tolerated her positivity and insane desire for us all to be close, but I can't do it anymore.

'My mum and Michelle,' Amalia continues, 'took Lily and me on trips all the time. I have the best memories of those holidays. Our kids are going to love it.'

'They're not even six months old,' I snap. 'We're not your Michelle.' My cheeks burn.

'What?' she says softly.

'I know you want us to be close single mums like your mum and Michelle. But it's never going to happen. We are forced to be friends, or acquaintances, because of what you did.'

'We've all broken the law by keeping this secret,' Amalia says.

'We did that for you. For Lila. You owe us,' I say. 'Now I don't want anything from you. I'm happy to catch up for mothers' group. But we aren't best friends and we never will be.'

Amalia blinks a few times and takes a deep breath. 'Right.'

'We should probably go,' I say. Fleur and I pick up our babies and leave.

Epilogue

Amalia

'Bye sweetheart,' I say to Lila as I drop her off at day care. 'I love you.'

The educator takes her from my arms, and I plant one last kiss on her forehead. I hate leaving her, but I need to work. It's part of my new plan to fulfil my mum's dying wish.

That day at my house six months ago was the last time I saw or spoke to Marnie. I was furious. Everything I'd done had been for her. For Peyton. I freed them of that cheating scumbag, and in the process, saved Fleur too. I should be their hero, their saviour. But they threw it back in my face. Michelle would never have betrayed my mum like that.

I drive past Fleur's house on my way to work. There's a 'Sold' sticker up on the 'For Sale' sign now. *Good for her*. Marnie and Peyton are still in town, but I never see them. Lakesfield isn't a big town. It often feels as though maybe they see me and hide. Or there is a whole section of Lakesfield undiscovered to me that they hang out in so as to not run into me.

After that day, I was back at square one. I almost considered taking Marcus back. I didn't know how I'd gotten to this stage of my life. A year ago I was in love. I was in a happy relationship and starting to announce to people that I was pregnant. Now, I was a lonely murderer.

When I killed Rob, I honestly thought I was doing them a favour. I wanted them to see that they were strong, and that they'd be fine without him. Like my mum. And it was the thoughts of my mum that reminded me that taking back Marcus was a bad idea. She'd be so ashamed of me.

Instead, I turned my focus to getting a job. I work three days a week at one of the pharmacies in town. I manage the accounts and order products, as well as working on the counter. I enjoy it and I get to talk to lots of people. Every day is filled with anticipation about who I might meet.

I open the pharmacy and begin unpacking the stock that arrived late yesterday. I carry a huge box of vitamins over to one of the shelves. Someone rushes over to me. I didn't hear the door open, and my pulse quickens at how quickly they approach me. *Was I being attacked?* I brace for impact. The person takes the box from my hands.

'Let me take that. It looks heavy,' he says.

'It's fine,' I respond even though it seems to weigh a ton.

He takes it from my arms anyway and now I can see him properly. He has kind brown eyes, ruffled red hair and looks incredibly hot in his tradie gear. 'I'm Paul, here to fix the plumbing in the staff kitchen.'

I smile. 'Follow me, Paul.'

I have a new plan.

Acknowledgements

Where do I start? So many people have helped me get to this point.

Firstly, I want to thank my readers for taking a chance on a new author and making this book lover a book writer. I hope you enjoyed this story and what's to come.

To my husband for supporting me and encouraging me to step outside my comfort zone. I couldn't have done any of this without you.

To my beautiful kids who inspire me every day. Most of this book was written *While the Baby Sleeps* so thanks for being legendary nappers.

To my family and in-laws for their support, encouragement and babysitting skills.

To Grandma and Old-Grandie who are and were writers before me and passed down their passion for storytelling, and to Grandie for sharing his favourite books with me.

To Elle, who pushed me into my first writing course, has read everything I've written, and pumps me up every day. She's my personal cheerleader.

To my critique readers—Bec, Elle and Emma—for making this story what it is. I'm so grateful for the time you have invested in reading my work. And to Maddie for her expertise when solving crimes.

Big thanks to my girls in the Beta Book Club, a group of beautiful fellow writers, who keep me motivated and entertained every week.

To my own mothers' group. No, we didn't cover up a murder but we entered motherhood together during the pandemic, and these women were an incredible support in the early days.

Thank you to my editors Kylie Mason and Laura Boon. I've learnt so much about storytelling and pesky English from you both.

To all my writer and reader friends, in real life and online, I'm so appreciative of your love, support and inspiration.

About the Author

Stephanie Hazeltine is a contemporary fiction author who writes about fearless females as they fall in love, navigate motherhood or tackle mysteries.
She lives in Melbourne, Australia with her husband, two kids and two cavoodles.

Sign up to her mailing list to be the first to know about new releases and exclusive news.
Website: www.stephaniehazeltine.com
Instagram: @stephaniehazeltinewrites
TikTok: @stephaniehazeltinewrites

ALSO BY STEPHANIE HAZELTINE

Suburban Secrets Series

While the Baby Sleeps

You Weren't Watching. Read it now

Standalones

The Retreat. A twisty thriller featuring an influencer and a stunning Australian resort. Read it now

Anthologies

Anyone But Him - a spicy, enemies-to-lovers collection of novellas. Read it <u>now</u>

All I Want for Chris-mas – a spicy holiday romance featuring Hollywood's hottest man. Read it now

www.ingramcontent.com/pod-product-compliance
Lightning Source LLC
Chambersburg PA
CBHW030617120726
47904CB00006B/1938